A Fine Madness

HIGHLAND BRIDES, BOOK 3

ELIZABETH ESSEX

A FINE MADNESS
Copyright © 2016 by Elizabeth Essex
Excerpt from *Mad for the Marquess,* Elizabeth Essex, 2016
Cover design by Patricia Schmitt/PickyMe Artist
Cover photo by Jenn LeBlanc/Studio Smexy
Vector images used under Creative Commons Attribution License: BSGStudio on All-Free-Download; Webdesignhot on All-Free-Download

ERB Publishing

ISBN: 978-0-9969881-9-3
For information, address Elizabeth Essex at elizabethessex.com

PRAISE FOR ELIZABETH ESSEX'S NOVELS

MAD FOR LOVE

"It's a fast-paced quick read that simply sparkles; the writing is deft and humorous." - *All About Romance*

MAD ABOUT THE MARQUESS

"This book is delightful…the dialogue is wonderful and sass wars are just about my favorite thing ever. The plot is just enough crazysauce layered on top of historical goodness. There was literally nothing about Mad About the Marquess that I didn't like." - *Smart B*tches, Trashy Books*, A Review

THE PURSUIT OF PLEASURE

"Elizabeth Essex's The Pursuit of Pleasure is elegant, evocative, and absolutely dangerous to a good night's sleep." -NY Times Bestseller *Courtney Milan*

ALMOST A SCANDAL

"*Almost a Scandal* eschews the balls, gowns, and clever conversation that characterize most Regency romances. But the love affair between Sally Kent, midshipman, and David Colyear, lieutenant, is utterly engrossing and (once Sally and David are sent on a mission to engage the French navy) thrilling as well." –*Eloisa James*, NY Times Bestselling Author

A SCANDAL TO REMEMBER

"Set sail with Essex as she cleverly pits a bluestocking against a stiff-upper-lipped British naval officer and lets the sparks fly. Essex spices her fast-paced tale with fascinating details of ships and sailing and adds plenty of sexual tension, high-seas adventures, danger and desire. Readers will be on the edges of their seats reading this latest Reckless Brides tale." – *Romantic Times*, 4 ½ stars and TOP PICK!

BOOKS BY ELIZABETH ESSEX

Dartmouth Brides
The Pursuit of Pleasure
A Sense of Sin
The Danger of Desire

Highland Brides
Mad for Love
Mad About the Marquess
A Fine Madness

The Kent Brothers Chronicles
Between the Devil and the Deep Blue Sea

Reckless Brides
Almost a Scandal
A Breath of Scandal
Scandal in the Night
The Scandal Before Christmas
After the Scandal
A Scandal to Remember

Anthologies
Vexed (*Between the Devil and the Deep Blue Sea*)
Scandal's Daughters (*A Fine Madness*)
Christmas Brides (*The Scandal Before Christmas*)

Chapter 1

Twelve Mile Burn Village
Midlothian, Scotland
June, 1792

ELSPETH OTIS HAD never particularly liked birthdays. And she liked her four and twentieth such day even less. Because this birthday came with something more than the usual disappointingly practical gift—this birthday brought her the unwanted gift of spinsterhood.

Such an ugly, unforgiving word, spinster—full of pity and dismissal and unfulfilled promise, all of which came to her in the form of the present of a lace cap, frilly and delicate, handmade by the Aunts, for whom spinsterhood was more a point of pride than a burden. But Elspeth felt the gossamer weight settle upon her like a stray cobweb stretched across the garden—unseen, unavoidable, and somehow inevitable.

How was she to avoid spinsterhood living with her aged aunts—the sisters Murray, as they were known—in a tiny thatched cottage, at the bitter end of a lane, in a forgotten village at the end of the world? How was she to avoid joining the Aunts irrevocably on the shelf?

"Put it on," urged Aunt Isla.

Elspeth could not. Only women of a *certain age* wore caps.

And unmarried women who put on caps were all but saying they had given up hope of ever finding love—given up believing that true love existed.

Elspeth did not want to give up hope, even if the idea of finding true love seemed as far-fetched as finding a pot of gold hidden in the garden—something she daydreamed about all the time, but which was never going to happen.

She held the fine lace creation up to the light and attempted to make appropriately admiring sounds. "So very pretty," she managed.

Really, it was pretty—fine and delicate and exquisite as spun sugar. And yet she could not bring herself to put it on her head. She racked her brain for a suitable excuse—anything would do. Anything that wouldn't hurt any finer feelings or seem ungrateful.

A sound came from without—the jangle of harness and the creak of cartwheels on the rutted track running up to the cottage.

"Someone's in the lane." Which was both a mercy and a true diversion—normally no carriages stopped at Dove Cottage. But Elspeth meant to make the most of the distraction, even if it were just a drover who had lost his way. Anything to put off the inevitable.

She pushed the lace cap deep into the pocket of her practical quilted skirts and bolted for the door. "I'll just have a wee look, shall I?"

"Elspeth!" Aunt Isla remonstrated. "Have a care!"

This was Elspeth's task in life—to have a care. To keep vigilant against all manner of mischief or mischance lurking within and without. To never call attention to herself, nor give up her guard against her tainted blood. To keep safe, and quiet, and not—under any circumstances—to be herself.

"Don't rush," Aunt Isla continued to complain. "Why must you always rush?"

Elspeth rushed because she was trying to outrace the dreadful dullness of her life. But also because a clarty, mud-splattered dray was drawing up beside their gate, and the driver was looking meaningfully at their cottage.

She was down the path in a trice, despite the dreich, dripping June weather.

The Aunts came hard behind, hovering in the cover of the doorway to listen to every word, so Elspeth was rather more careful of her diction—no scaffy, vulgar Scots cant for the genteel sisters Murray—than her skirts. "May I help you?"

"Deliv'ry fer Mizz Otis," bawled the driver over the chitter of the rain, shooting his thumb over his shoulder at the large tarpaulin-covered mound in the muddy well of his dray.

"There must be a mistake. We're expecting no deliveries," Aunt Molly called from the doorway, waving her arm to shoo the nuisance of a man away, as if he were a large, mud-splattered midge.

But the dray man was stout of heart as well as of girth, and assessed the situation with one squinted eye. His gaze pegged square on Elspeth. "Ye be Mizz Otis?"

"Aye. I am Miss Otis." Elspeth stepped through the gate into the rutted lane, not caring if she did get soaking drookit—she was as stout-hearted as any other Scots lass, and she was more curious than she was afraid of catching cold. "What is it you're delivering?" She went on tiptoe to peer over the side. "From whom is it sent?"

The mystery was better than anything she might have imagined, lulling herself to sleep at night with adventures and fairy tales, or daydreaming her way through the endless round of chores.

The driver heaved his bulk down onto the lane. "Frae Edinburgh," was his terse answer. "Sn' Andrew Square."

Elspeth was utterly enchanted—nothing so exciting had ever happened to her before.

"Nay!" Aunt Isla cried. The driver's words doused her aunts more effectively than any downpour—they shrank back into the doorway, as if the dray might contain some great calamity instead of what was undoubtedly some commonplace item—for nothing outside of commonplace had ever occurred in their village.

The driver barely raised a bushy brow. "A trunk, it be," he went on as he began untying ropes and peeling back the tarpaulin to reveal the most battered, unprepossessing, commonplace old trunk Elspeth had ever seen. "Where d'ye want it?"

"I'm no sure." Besides the fact that Elspeth could not imagine how or why she should be sent a trunk from Edinburgh, her aunts' reactions told her they would be loath to allow the thing into the cottage. "What does it contain?"

"Iniquity!" Aunt Isla's thin voice was sharp with frantic accusation. "She needs nothing from that huzzy. Nothing, I tell you! Take it back, take it back."

Elspeth had rarely heard such pointed invective from the Aunts. "What huzzy?"

The Aunts exchanged one of their long moments of silent communication before it was somehow tacitly decided that Aunt Molly would answer. "*That Wastrel's* sister," she said at last, pursing her thin lips in distaste. "She has a house, so we are told, on St. Andrew Square in Edinburgh."

That Wastrel being her late, unlamented father. Of whom Elspeth was never to speak.

"Den of vipers," Isla added in a fervent whisper. "All of a piece."

A piece of what, Elspeth did not ask. She was too busy overcoming the curious shock of learning she had any other kin in the world besides the two elderly relations in front of her, let alone a woman who lived so close as Edinburgh. The metropolis was a little over twelve miles to the north and east, but for Elspeth, who had never been allowed to venture farther than the next wee village, it might as well have been the farthest reaches of the heathen Americas.

"Why in heaven's name did you never tell me?"

"Because a more scandalous, scarlet woman of Babylon never lived," was Isla's fervent opinion.

"We thought it best," was Molly's more decorous judgment.

"But she, this scarlet woman"—and if a lass were to have an unknown relation, how intriguing, and somehow inevitable, that she should be a scarlet woman—"has known of me? Well, clearly she has." Elspeth answered her own question. "For she has sent me a present. On my birthday. But how strange that she should never have written me before."

Another fraught, stony-faced look passed silently between the two elderly sisters.

"Aunt Molly?" Elspeth faced the eldest of the two. "Do you mean to tell me she *has* written to me previously?"

"We thought it best," Molly repeated, "to keep you from the influence—"

"—the iniquitous influence," Isla amended.

"—of *that Wastrel*'s family."

Elspeth braced herself for the lecture she knew would be coming following the mention of her long-dead father. John Otis had done three things to earn the sobriquet of *that Wastrel.* Firstly, he had fallen in love with her mother, the Aunts' lovely youngest sister, Fiona, which had led to pregnancy, Elspeth's birth, and shortly thereafter, her mother's untimely death. Secondly, he had written a book so scandalous, licentious and popular that it had subsequently been banned from publication. And lastly, he had, in his grief over his young wife's death, slowly drunk himself to death, leaving his only daughter to the tender care of the only family she had left in the world—her devoted, but strict, spinster aunts.

"We wanted to wait until you were older," Aunt Molly tried to explain.

"Old enough to know better," Isla added.

Well. Elspeth was certainly old enough now, wasn't she, now that she was a dashed spinster?

"There be a letter, too." The dray man slapped a thick, expensively papered letter with Elspeth's own name in an elegant scrawl across the front into her palm.

"Michty me." Elspeth gave vent to her astonishment with forbidden Scots cant. "What else have ye twa been keeping frae me?"

Chapter 2

"I'M SURE YOU know why I've called you here, Hamish."

Hamish Cathcart, third, last legitimate, but unfortunately not forgotten son of the Earl Cathcart, did not know why his father had summoned him to the dark-paneled book room of his Edinburgh townhouse. Nor did he particularly care. His father's summons only ever amounted to one thing—Hamish was to shut his smart mouth and do as he was bid.

Which he did do. Sometimes.

Sometimes he played the dutiful third son, and obeyed. And sometimes he only gave the appearance of obeisance, and quietly found a way to do what he wanted without ruffling the earl's carefully preened feathers.

Today, however, was not going to be one of those times. Because today he had a very strong hunch he knew exactly what the auld man was working himself into a fine lather to say—Hamish was going to be cut off.

So be it.

"You can't think I intend to finance you all of your days. And you can't expect that after I'm gone, your brother, William, will simply pay you an allowance indefinitely."

On this point, Hamish did agree with the tightfisted auld bean. He did *not* think his allowance—indifferently given and indifferently received—would continue indefinitely. Which was why he had never spent the money his father doled out to him as the auld man assumed, on cheap wine, cheaper women and off-key song. Hamish had, instead, quite prudently, invested it.

But with investment came risk. And although risk had its rewards, it also had its downfalls.

At the moment, Hamish's finances had rather fallen down.

Yet he was more than sure that he could revive himself, just as he always had, and make another modest fortune. An idea was poised at the back of his brain—poised and not entirely formed. Not without—

"—a wife."

Ye gods. Hamish's wayward attention snapped back to the auld badger. "I beg your pardon?"

"Do you hear nothing I say?"

"I distinctly heard you say the word 'wife'." Hamish pronounced the word with the same wariness he reserved for "serpent" or "debutante" or "debt collector."

"Indeed." The earl slapped the flat of his palm against the desktop, as if that explained everything. "You need a wife. With a suitable fortune. Luckily, you've got your hair and your teeth, if not a great deal of ambition or steadiness of character, so we ought to be able to take a good pick of the available heiresses. I've drawn up a list—"

"We?" Hamish didn't care if his tone was swimming in sarcasm.

A sarcasm his father willfully ignored. "Of course your mother will have her candidates as well, but I should think I know far better what a young man of your character requires, eh?" The earl allowed himself a chuckle. "I've my eye on a few fillies that should take your fancy enough to make it no chore to get an heir off her."

Hamish shoved the distasteful idea of equating a lass to a brood mare out of his mind, consigning it to the rubbish heap that was the only suitable receptacle for his father's crude, patronizing view of the world. "As I am not *the heir*, I've no need to get myself one."

When that pleasantly snide observation elicited no

discernible reaction, Hamish tried the prick of a more pointed probe. "And need I remind you of the unhappy state of your own arranged marriage? You're hardly a recommendation for such an arrangement."

His father looked down his impressively long nose. "Don't be crass."

"And arranging to take a lass to wife with the same callous calculation as if she were a mare at a fair is not? I am not being crass, but factual." Even if Hamish and his siblings had not been witness to years and years of continuous marital sniping and discord, Hamish's illegitimate half-brother, Rory, was proof enough of their father's infidelity.

And yet his father called Hamish unsteady.

His father was not best pleased at this display of logic. "And what, you fancy yourself in *love?*" This time it was his father's voice that dripped with sarcasm.

"Heaven forfend," Hamish laughed off the idea—he might be unsteady, but he was not unhinged. "Not at all, sir." He was too busy for anything so time-consuming as love. "I have other plans to secure my future that do not require shackling myself to some unknown lass."

"Better someone unknown," his father advised darkly, "than someone for whom you've too much regard."

Though he was no poetry-spouting romantic, Hamish immediately rejected such a dismal view. He had friends enough with good marriages—the aforementioned half-brother, Rory, and his lovely French wife, Mignon, came immediately to mind—to know that regard for one's partner in life was not only preferable, it was positively necessary. "That is your opinion, sir. I, myself, will not contemplate marriage without it."

But the sad truth of the matter was that there was no lass for whom he felt such regard. No one at all.

"So be it." His father stood. "From this day forward, I am done with you. The ledger"—he clapped the account book open before him shut—"is closed. If you care not for the benefit of my advice and counsel on the matter of getting a wife, I will leave you to the dubious pleasure of your mother's *tender*"—his tone carried all the weight of his distaste for his wife of thirty years—"cares. Good luck with any wife *she* might find for you. Prim, priggish lasses like she's made your sisters—so missish they could curdle milk with their sour looks."

As Hamish would rather be made to walk naked down Edinburgh's High Street than spend two minutes with any such woman, he softened his tone. "Forgive me, Father, if I appeared ungrateful. But I simply don't share your urgency for my marriage. I am not so done up without your money that I don't have a feather to fly by. Far from it. I am not so frivolous or imprudent as that."

Indeed, he had not been frivolous at all—he had just had a run of bad luck, was all. Yet he was sure he could revive his fortunes sufficiently to make marrying for money entirely unnecessary.

But his father knew nothing of Hamish's business ventures. And Hamish intended to keep it that way— gentlemen, even unsteady third sons of earls, did not engage openly in trade. Nothing would be surer to ruin his prospects like the scandal of the earl's son dirtying his hands with work.

"You have until Whitsunday to pick a bride. Your mother will like a June wedding." Earl Cathcart flicked an imaginary bit of fluff off his immaculate sleeve before he regarded his son through narrowed eyes. "If you're smart—though I see little sign of being so—you'll avail yourself of this list of gels"—he thrust a sheet of foolscap at Hamish—"before your mother provides you with a suitably prim list of her own. Believe me, even if she's never spoken of it, she has one."

Unfortunately, his mother had, indeed, spoken of it—a son did not reach the recklessly dangerous age of eight and twenty without his mother offering the name of at least one "suitable" miss. "I understand you, sir."

"Good." The earl crossed the room and held open the door. "Whitsunday."

Hamish placed his hat on his head, pulling the tricorn down low, so his father could not see the hot flare of scorn in his eyes.

Whitsunday was less than five weeks away—an entirely ridiculous deadline. But Hamish would beat it.

Bollocks to Whitsunday.

<h1 style="text-align:center">Chapter 3</h1>

WHAT THE AUNTS had kept from her was the astonishing fact that Lady Augusta Ivers, her father's sister, had, for four and twenty years, sent not only birthday greetings, but also yearly invitations for her niece to visit—invitations which the sisters Murray had always declined. But this year, the canny lady had sent something besides the invitation—the trunk—which was too big for the Aunts to hide.

Elspeth stared at both the trunk and the now-opened letter. It was as if she had awoken to find a tame unicorn in the garden. To think that all these years—all these years she had worked so hard to stifle her indecorous curiosity, to keep her idle daydreaming to herself and be content with her paltry lot—she might have seen something of the world beyond the confines of her small, muddy corner of Midlothian.

In the lane, the dray man hefted the big trunk as if it were as light as kindling. "Where d'ye want it put?"

"Not inside! We've no room—" Isla shut the door against both the trunk and the eyes of curious neighbors, who had begun to gather by the gate.

Elspeth felt her heart plummet straight from her chest to land with a splat on her muddy shoes. "Michty me." What good was a present from a mysterious, scarlet aunt if she could not even accept it to find out what lay inside?

"If ye don' want it"—the dray man shrugged—"I've direction to take it back. Paid for tha' at t'other end, herself did."

"Herself?"

"Leddy Augusta Ivers, as they was talking aboot." The dray man balanced the load on one broad shoulder. "She sayed as I wus to gie it ye, or bring it straight back tae herself."

"Could you take *me* back with it?" The words were out of her mouth before Elspeth could even gather the presence of mind to wish them back.

But she didn't wish them back. She wanted to go. She had never wanted anything so much in her entire life.

"Please." She spoke both more firmly and more politely this time, even though her heart was clattering in her ear like the off-balance spinning wheel in the corner of the parlor. "I'd be sore obliged if you would please take me with you."

"Tae Edinburgh?" The driver's bushy eyebrows rose up, poised in consideration.

Elspeth was shocked by her own temerity in standing up for herself—of daring to want something that had seemed so far out of reach for so long, the possibility of which hadn't even existed until a moment ago—but she held her rain-splattered ground. "You do go straight back to Edinburgh, do you not?"

"Aye."

Her heart spun faster—she had to convince him or perhaps forever lose her chance. "Could you not easily take me there as well?"

The driver stroked the grizzled ends of his ginger whiskers in contemplation. "I s'pose I could. Fer a price."

And here was the fox concealed in the henhouse—Elspeth had absolutely no ready money of her own. But she did have ready wits. "Lady Ivers already paid you to bring me the trunk, and bring it back, did she not? If you take me with it, as she asks in her letter"—Elspeth pretended to consult the missive from Lady Ivers as if it did verily contain such a request—"Lady Ivers will surely reward you handsomely for the service."

This was a rather delicate piece of fibbery, but Elspeth was prepared to risk the mortal sin for the potential reward of escaping her stifling village and her stifling life.

Of escaping spinsterhood.

Mercifully, the dray man warmed to the idea. "Aye. She might at that. Well, come ye on then."

Relief and excitement made a tangled skein of her insides. "Will you bide here a short while, so I can gather my things?"

And do the hardest thing yet—tell the Aunts what she had done.

The driver turned his squint to the sky, as if gauging the hours of daylight left. "No more'n t'irty minutes," he warned. "Or I'll g'on without ye."

"I'll be back," she swore. "So help me, I will."

The Aunts were waiting just inside the door in forbearance of another of Elspeth's unseemly displays of rash behavior, though they could have no idea just how rash she had truly been. Or how rash she was yet prepared to be.

"Elspeth," Molly chided. "Mind your skirts and boots. You're covered in mud."

"I'm not coming in for more than a moment." There was nothing for it but to give them the uncomfortable truth. "I've asked the dray man to take me to Edinburgh. To Lady Ivers."

The tight-lipped silence that greeted this proposal told Elspeth exactly what the Aunts thought of such an idea even before they erupted in speech.

"Are you run mad? You cannot want to go to *her*." Aunt Molly's shocked tone allowed it to be impossible.

"She can't want you," was Isla's less kind answer.

Elspeth deflected the cutting remark as if it were an errant spindle needle—her aunt's inflammatory but impotent jabs had long become too dull a weapon to truly hurt her now. "But she does want me. She says so in her letter. And after all these years of so *faithfully*"—she chose a word her Aunts could not depreciate—"writing to me without response, I feel I must answer, and even atone, for my years of silence." Years of silence that her aunts knew could be laid at their feet.

"That's hardly necessary," Aunt Molly began with an

attempt at a polite but grim sort of logic.

"Because she's hardly decent!" Isla was too scandalized to admit any logic. "She's wicked."

Elspeth disagreed as politely as possible. "She seems very decent, as well as civil and ladylike, in her letter."

"That is as may be"—Aunt Molly was clearly searching for excuses—"but I'm not sure that it is advisable...or proper."

"Why?"

Aunt Molly's pale face colored, as if she could hardly bring herself to answer. "The lady is of...dubious moral fiber— thrice-married and thrice conveniently widowed."

"Those Otises. Bad blood, the lot of them," was Isla's more unguarded opinion.

As "the lot of them" included Elspeth and her own tainted share of the blood her late, unlamented father had bequeathed her, she felt the need to defend the family. "Lady Augusta can hardly be held to account for her husbands dying. Or is it that you think she's had more than her fair share of them?"

The moment the hasty, unkind words were out of her mouth, Elspeth bit her lips together as if she could swallow such ungrateful meanness of spirit whole and unspoken. Her Aunts had sacrificed to raise her, and had kept her out of love—a stifling version of love, but love nonetheless.

But Molly, bless her, was equal to the truth. "Perhaps, Elspeth. Yes. You are right that not all of our circumstances are the product of choice. Sometimes one must take what life offers, and simply make the best of it."

Heat scratched at the back of Elspeth's eyes—the Aunts had, indeed, made the best of it all—their genteel poverty due to absence of opportunities, lack of education, and reduced circumstances. But she could not give in to the choking pity. Not now, when it felt as if the whole of her life depended upon it. When opportunity was so close. "Then perhaps you understand that I might wish for a change in my circumstances, at least for a short visit. Just this once."

Because before she put on the lace cap of the spinster, and consigned herself forevermore to their forgotten corner of their Scotland, Elspeth Otis had a few things she meant to do—if true love had not come to Twelve Mile Burn to find her, she meant to go out into the wide world, and find love for herself.

Chapter 4

HAMISH STRODE UP the damp, stone staircase out of the Princes Street Gardens, taking the steps two at a time. He had to keep moving—he always thought better on his feet, with the wind in his face and an idea between his teeth. It might take him all day to climb to the top of Calton Hill, or even Arthur's Seat, but by the time he arrived at the top, he was sure to have thought of a solution to his rather dire dilemma.

"Hamish Cathcart?" A woman's voice penetrated the fog wreathing his brain. "Why, you're just the young man I need to see. Where are you off to in such an all-fired rush?"

Hamish turned to find Lady Augusta Ivers at the bottom of the stairs, and retraced his steps. "My dear Lady Ivers." He bowed over the hand the elegantly-clad widow offered him. "Delighted, as always, to see you, my lady."

Lady Augusta Ivers was a well-known fixture in Edinburgh's society, as admired as she was universally liked. She could always be counted upon to have some fresh and interesting intelligence about Edinburgh and the world—her circle of friends and correspondents extended to the continent and beyond.

"Well enough," she answered in her usual polished, self-possessed way. "But enough social palaver. You are just the man I was hoping to see. I have been meaning to speak to you about a proposition I think might suit both of us equally."

Hamish was instantly leery—in his eight and twenty years he had entertained any number of "propositions" from widowed ladies. But he had never thought Lady Ivers the type—although younger than her late husband, she had been entirely devoted to Admiral Ivers. "How may I be of service to you, my lady?"

"A business proposition, Hamish, my lad. Not that I'm not flattered." Lady Ivers flashed him a knowing but kind smile. "Have you an office where we might speak privately?"

He did not. At present, Hamish conducted his business in a corner chair at Smyth's Coffee House off the Grass Market, but such an establishment was hardly the place for a lady, even one as unflappable as Augusta Ivers.

"Never mind." The lady was already waving him off, impatient to get to her point. "Walk with me, where we might not be overheard." She took his arm, and led him back the way he had come, into the privacy of the garden paths. "It has recently come to my attention that the publishing house of Prufrock & Company is in some financial difficulty. This distresses me, as they were the publisher of my late brother's entirely scandalous, but entirely popular novel."

"Aye, my lady?" Hamish was familiar with the work. Indeed, any lad who had been to university in Scotland was familiar with the tale of Fanny Bahoochie—and there was a particularly apt name for the protagonist of *A Memoir of a Game Girl*. Sweet, game Fanny Bahoochie had been the stuff of schoolboy fantasy.

But how this might matter to him now, Hamish knew not.

Lady Ivers was keen to inform him. "I have been thinking of commissioning a new version of my late brother's work to bring to publication. A considerably less scandalous version, retaining all of the charm, but a great deal less of the salacious content of the original."

As far as Hamish was concerned, the charm of the original had been in the salacious content—at least it had been for the young gentleman readers at Saint Andrew's University.

"If the book were in the *right* hands," the lady continued

to explain, "Prufrock—who still holds the rights to publish, you see—could make a fortune. As could others who stand to benefit. The work is notorious enough to still be well known—it would sell itself if Prufrock had enough talent and vision to create a version that would pass the censors. But Prufrock lacks both imagination and, to be frank, ready money."

Ye gods.

A marvelous sort of sensation started at the back of his brain—the sort of tingling sensation that could not be ignored. The sort of sensation that had made—and lost— him several fortunes.

This time, he was determined to be prudent. "How much money?"

Lady Ivers gifted him with a pleased, knowing smile. "I like you, Hamish. You're clever and quick. You understand."

Aye, he understood. He could practically taste the possibility—sharp and potent like good Scots whisky.

She named a goodly sum. "Have you the blunt?"

He didn't. Not all of it. But most.

Because Augusta Ivers was as sharp as they came—her acumen and head for investments were well known amongst her set. And Hamish was already acquainted with Prufrock & Company, Publisher and Fine Press, suppliers of high quality volumes of poetry—he had purchased a collection a time or two. The company was comprised of one Abel Prufrock, ancient but well-respected publisher, one articled clerk to mind the books, one pressman to mind the printing, and two gawking apprentices to mind the pressman—already a lean, if not presently profitable enterprise. It occupied a small but efficient premises at the end of Fowl's Close, which curved like a short, lower rib off the long spine of the High Street, down the back of the city.

"You see it, don't you?" Lady Ivers pressed. "How their fortunes might be reversed with an infusion of cash which would allow them to print the new version of Fanny's story? How the right man might reshape that novel into something more palatable and acceptable to the general public, not to mention the censors?"

He did see. He also saw the flaw in such a seemingly simple plan—finding the right man to tame the more erotic episodes of the story into something merely racy, and pep up the mundane bits to something livelier. He had no idea if he could be that man. But still, the idea had merit. And potential. But he would also need to speak with Abel Prufrock personally, and look at the books, and see if it really would take as much blunt as Lady Ivers estimated.

It was as if she could read his mind. "My information is impeccable, but Prufrock may be willing to negotiate. If you think you can do it, I stand ready and willing to provide any additional capital—for a commensurate share of future profits, of course, as well as the increased sales income from the book—that might be needed. But I need a man like you to be Prufrock's partner, to see that things are done right, as they should be. That the book is revised well enough to make the fortune it ought."

A man like him.

And there it was—that fire in his belly that spread to his brain. That hunger for a new endeavor that had all the potential he might have hoped for. And he hadn't even had to climb all the way up to the top of Arthur's Seat—opportunity had come knocking at his own door.

But this was the first time opportunity had ever worn lavender silk.

Chapter 5

FOR A LASS who had never been farther from home than the edge of the village, each turn in the road, each fresh vista, was a revelation to Elspeth. She fancied the early summer sunshine made even the mud sparkle as the slow-moving dray afforded her a spectacular view of the Pennine Hills, which pointed like a huge earthen arrow toward the capital.

Four hours of slow travel brought them to the edge of the metropolis. To the north, the city seemed to rise up out of the earth like a stone dragon's spine beneath the high outcrop of the fabled Arthur's Seat, and what had to be the lush green parkland of the Holyrood Palace rolling away to the east.

Within the city, the streets were close and narrow and rattling with the deafening noise of a hundred horses' and oxen's hooves clattering along the slick, uneven cobbles. Elspeth could barely think for all the sound—she had never heard anything like it.

But mercifully for her ears, the dray man finally made his slow, laborious way into a quieter neighborhood—an oasis of calm, lined with new trees in their first bud hemming a neat, green garden square where he drew his team to a halt in front of the prettiest wedding cake of a stone townhouse Elspeth had ever seen.

After having spent a good portion of the long ride

imagining what a person of wicked disposition and dubious morals might look like, Elspeth was entirely unprepared for the elegant, refined woman in exquisite lavender silk who rushed out of the house to personally greet her on the steps of her equally elegant, refined townhouse.

"Oh, my darling niece!" The moment Elspeth stepped to the pavement, she found herself enveloped in a plushly scented embrace. "Oh, I would have known you anywhere! If you aren't the very image of your darling mother. Such a lass! Her smile could light up half of Edinburgh, and I collect that yours will light up the other half."

Elspeth was beyond astonished. And beyond pleased. In all of her four and twenty years, no one had ever said such a thing about her mother. Nor about her own smile.

But years of guarding herself against potential wickedness made Elspeth retreat from the effusive, warm embrace so she might make her aunt a properly restrained curtsey in greeting. "Lady Ivers. Thank you so very much for your kind invitation."

"You are very welcome. I own myself delighted that you were finally able to accept after all these years, even if it is a sudden surprise." Lady Ivers' infectious laugh spilled across the street. "I suppose the sisters Murray finally judged you to be past the age of danger?"

Elspeth felt her cheeks heat in the face of such insight. "Nay, milady. I came on my own say so," she confessed. "The Aunts Murray didn't approve."

"Gracious!" Lady Ivers clasped her hands in astonished delight. "How wonderfully intrepid of you, making the journey without help. Oh, but I am so glad you are finally come, my darling, darling girl. Such a wonderful surprise, but I am already making plans for you, my darling—to take you about as soon as may be, to show you the sights, and show the sights you!"

Lady Ivers linked her arm with Elspeth's to escort her into the entry room full of dramatic, polished black and white marble, but Elspeth had no time to gape like the greenling she was, for as soon as she was divested of her country cloak by a very refined attendant maid, her lady aunt swept her up the curved stairs to a drawing room furnished in such a perfectly stunning shade of water blue, Elspeth felt her breath soar out of her throat in wonder.

The house was like something out of a dream—Elspeth had never even seen such glossy, tissue-thin silks at the drapers in the village. No one in their fusty hamlet could even have call for such a sumptuous fabric, let alone the coin to purchase such luxurious lengths as were cascading from the tall, clear-paned windows.

Who knew iniquity would look so fine?

"My poor lamb, you must be utterly exhausted." Lady Augusta put a gentle hand to Elspeth's face. "We must have some refreshment for you."

"Thank you, my lady. You are all kindness."

"Nonsense. I haven't a kind bone in my body," the lady claimed while her angelic smile countered her argument. "I trust the Murray sisters will have thoroughly warned you against me."

Elspeth must have looked conscious, for Lady Ivers laughed. "Well, it is some comfort to know they have not changed a spit, however they have annoyed me by denying me your company. But now we must make up for lost time— I know so little about you. You must tell me all."

"There is little to tell, my lady. We live at home, quiet and retired."

"Such a waste of youth," the lady tsked. "I don't know how I will ever forgive them, except to make up for lost time. Though you have lived quietly, do you think you should like to go about and see a little of society?"

Elspeth could scarcely believe her good fortune, though she strove mightily not to be overwhelmed by it. "With you to help and guide me, my lady."

"Just so. You are so like her." Lady Ivers was all happy, suppressed tears. "Your mother—I see her face when I look at you. And just as intrepid, I should surmise, to have come all this way alone, without permission." Lady Ivers let out a happy sigh. "So, what do you think of the city—your mother's city—upon first impression?"

"The city is everything interesting and exciting, my lady, I thank you. Though I confess I also find it rather loud and very dirty."

"Yes, I imagine you might after an overly quiet life in the country."

Elspeth realized her life had been more than quiet—it had been small. Dove Cottage was all she had known, but in the easy elegance of Lady Ivers' garden of a home, she began to feel the prickles and thorns that might have grown on her character along with the roses that rambled up the walls of the auld cottage.

"But Auld Reeky, as we natives call Edinburgh, isn't so bad, once you get to know her," Lady Ivers assured Elspeth, while holding out a cup and saucer. "Sugar?"

"No, I thank you, my lady." Elspeth had never acquired a taste for sweets, growing up in a house with such strict economies that sugar was considered a luxury.

"You must call me Aunt." Lady Augusta smiled and handed her the cup. "It would mean so much to me."

"Thank you, Aunt Augusta." Elspeth took a reviving sip of the strong, hot tea, grateful that this aunt did not seem to have to reuse her tea leaves until they could no longer color the water. "That's full delicious."

"Excellent! I must warn you I plan on spoiling you wonderfully, so you'll have no thought of going home. Which will be a difficult task, I'll warrant—I've no doubt you're brimming with staunch moral fiber after having been brought up by the sisters Murray."

"You know my aunts?"

"Oh, yes. We all grew up together, your mother, your father, your aunts and I, though I will point out that I was the youngest." A wonderfully mischievous twinkle lighted her eyes. "And the one, they will have told you, with the most of the devil in me, though I am sure they will gainsay your father his share. The 'devil's cubs' they called us, and did their best to keep your mother away from our influence. But that only made the nectar of forbidden fruit the sweeter for her. Ah, she was the loveliest girl, your mother. I can see you take after her in that way." Aunt Augusta smiled and squeezed Elspeth's hand again in reassurance. "So you, my dear, must of course stay here as long as you should like."

Elspeth's relief was more than profound—she felt as if she could draw breath for the first time in hours. "Thank you, Aunt Augusta. That is very generous of you."

"You are most welcome." She reached out a hand to gently touch Elspeth's face. "You know I have thought of you often—every day, in fact. All these years, wondering how you fared, wondering what you were like, if you looked like either of them? They were my greatest friends in the world, your mother and father."

Something stronger than gratitude made a lump in Elspeth's throat. "I was afraid you might be ashamed of your illegitimate niece."

"Illegitimate? Never! What nonsense. Who let you believe such a thing?" The lady's soft tone went calmly vehement. "Your parents loved each other, and were hand-fasted, which is perfectly legal even if it wasn't fine enough for the Murrays." Lady Ivers put her chin up, as if facing an unseen enemy. "If they told you that, they were—and are—wrong. Your parents were married."

Elspeth's eyes grew dangerously damp. "Thank you, Aunt Augusta." It was the kindest, most generous thing anyone had ever said to her.

"I shall box their ears, the sisters Murray, if ever I should see them again." Aunt Augusta closed her eyes, as if she couldn't bear to think of them. "So I must take care that I do not ever see them again, for I should so hate to act according to their prejudices! But enough of them and their spleen. I declare I am practically ravenous at the prospect of taking you about the town, for such a lovely girl will find no shortage of partners here in Edinburgh. You shall have your pick of the handsomest young gentlemen in no time."

Elspeth was more than astonished—she was hopeful. "Do you really think so?"

"Absolutely." Lady Augusta was confident. "You're just

the sort of pretty, intelligent lass a clever young gentleman likes to talk to. You'll see. Once we have our way with putting a bit of polish and dash to you, you'll be just the thing."

Elspeth hoped she would be *some* thing. Most devoutly.

Aunt Augusta had none of Elspeth's reservations, and quite a bit more of her hopefulness—she bore Elspeth up like a butterfly on a breeze. "But you must be exhausted from your journey and all my chatter, so let me show you to your room, and then I must go write some letters canceling my plans for the evening so we might dine quietly at home, just the two of us. I have so much to ask you, but I mustn't exasperate or tire you out."

"Oh, I am *very* well used to being exasperated, my lady." Too late Elspeth realized her unguarded speech was unkind. "Oh, michty me—I should never have said that."

"You darling girl. You may say and think as you like when you are with me—I insist upon it," Aunt Augusta laughed. "We shall make you into something of an outspoken bluestocking yet. But here we are." She threw open the door to a bedchamber. "What do you think?"

What Elspeth thought was that she must certainly be dreaming, for such an elegant spacious chamber was like something out of her imaginings of a less dreary world—even the walls were covered with soft, shimmering blue silk. "I think you must be like the magical godmother in the French fairy tales."

"You like it. I'm so very glad. Because I will confess that I've had it ready for you—made up with you in mind. All these years—four and twenty—though I have done it over once or twice along the way."

Elspeth could not possibly contain the tears that welled up in her eyes—tears of gratitude, and tears of love along with tears for all the years that she had missed.

"Oh, my darling, don't cry. Don't cry!" Aunt Augusta swept her into a comfortably tight embrace. "You are here now and need never leave if you don't want to. We'll unpack your trunks and settle you in permanently this very minute."

"But I haven't any trunks but the one you sent me, Aunt

Augusta," Elspeth sniffed. "I've only the clothes upon my back and a small valise." She pointed to the small bag into which she had hastily stuffed her few possessions before leaving Dove Cottage.

Elspeth's lack of both accouterments and refinement was as nothing to Lady Ivers—she waved the difficulty away with a scented handkerchief. "Then my first letter shall be to my dressmaker. And in the meantime, my dresser will delight in making over some gowns to suit you, see if she won't. But, my dear," Aunt Augusta asked, turning to the battered trunk that had already been delivered into the room, "does that mean you did not get a chance to open up my gift?"

"Oh!" Elspeth moved toward the dear old trunk that had been her companion on her journey. "Please don't think me ungrateful. It's just that there was no time—"

"Of course. You did the right thing to come when you could. But I think now, after my talk of dresses, that you will be sorely disappointed in the contents." Her aunt unlatched and lifted the heavy lid. "I wish I had some things of your mother's to give you, but this will have to do." She lifted a sheaf of foolscap tied in a bundle with twine. "It was your father's, the trunk, though it just contains some bits of his writings. But I thought you might like to have it."

"Oh, yes, please." While Elspeth might have been at least a little disappointed that the trunk did not contain sparkling gemstones and golden doubloons—as one might expect in any self-respecting treasure trunk sent by a mysterious benefactor—she was happy to have anything of her long-unlamented father. "I know so little of him."

Aunt Augusta sighed. "Poor man—brilliant but perhaps a trifle weak. Or just heartbroken. But his words are still the best of him. I've read my brother's writings many times over the years, and I always feel as if the words bring me closer to him. And I suppose I hoped they would bring you closer to him, as well. Even if they are a bit naughty, his stories. But you are well old enough to think and decide things for yourself now."

Elspeth could not help but smile at Aunt Augusta's serene

approach to the world. The Aunts Murray had always characterized her father's book as entirely unfit for tender eyes, and they had always characterized Elspeth as so flighty, so wrapped up in her febrile imagination that she was unfit to render her own judgments of things. Yet she *was* old enough to decide for herself. "I think I should like to read them."

"Then you shall. You must learn to think and do as you like, my dear."

Chapter 6

AND SO SHE did—in the busy, whirlwind days that followed, Elspeth returned again and again to the unfinished story in the trunk, reading a scene here and a chapter there in the quiet moments between visits to dressmakers and bookstores and milliners.

In the hubbub of the chattering, enchanting city, it was a private pleasure to lose herself in the quiet flow of words, to indulge her imagination in her father's half-finished story. Though she avoided some of the particularly carnal scenes, Elspeth amused herself by returning to other, less earthy portions, paging through the fragile sheets, letting the words lead her into different, newly imagined worlds, making up different, happier endings.

It was heaven—a heaven of her own making. And Aunt Augusta's making, too—her new aunt never nagged, never once told Elspeth to stop daydreaming and pay heed. It was almost as if Aunt Augusta were daydreaming, too, and reveled in the glorious peace and evocative quiet.

"Elspeth, my dear." Aunt Augusta's voice was everything unstudied and casual as they drank their breakfast chocolate—lovely, rich and decadent—one morning before heading out to be fitted at a shoemaker's. "You've had a chance now to read those bits of your father's writing—tell me, what did you think?"

"I thought a hundred things—all different. I think I've imagined a different ending every time."

"Have you? How wonderfully creative." Aunt Augusta smiled and laughed. "You are more like him—like your father—than I ever hoped. I confess I feared the sisters Murray had nagged the imagination right out of you. But I am glad to find they did not."

"You don't mind my flights of fancy, as they called them?"

"Heavens, no! So you didn't find the writing too…shall we say too piquant, too racy for your taste?"

Now that Elspeth was becoming a sophisticated woman of the world—for Edinburgh was an entirely enlightened, international city—she would pay no mind to the riddy heat that rose in her cheeks. Though it had been rather shocking to read the frankly carnal scenes in the story, it was doubly disconcerting to discuss such things out loud. But even though Elspeth knew she was well out of her depth, but she would not give in to embarrassment—she would discuss the topic as urbanely as Aunt Augusta.

And Elspeth reckoned she had read the pages without any lingering damage to her virtue. And she had liked it. "The part I have read, I found *picaresque*, I think is the word."

Aunt Augusta laughed merrily. "Oh, yes, that is exactly the word. Another word might be *naughty*. He had a delightfully irreverent view of the world, your father."

"Clearly." But Elspeth found herself hungry for any knowledge of the man she had only heard spoken of disparagingly. "But it's not all naughty, surely. Some passages are quite…elevating. And beautiful—lyrical and… I don't know what, but they send me off making up stories of my own."

"Yes, exactly so!" Aunt Augusta nodded with a sigh. "Quite brilliant. So very like him."

Elspeth caught a bit of her aunt's happy melancholy. "I had no idea he was brilliant as well as…naughty."

"Made a villain of him, did they, the sisters Murray? No, don't defend them." Aunt Augusta looked out the window and smiled at her memories. "Your father was brilliant but…different. A bit difficult. Life wasn't always easy for him—for us. We weren't born into wealth. You father won his way through his own merit—he was a scholar, chosen for his cleverness, at the Cathedral school of St. Giles." She closed her eyes. "I can see him now, bounding away up those worn steps. We had to stay behind, your mother Fie and I, for we were lasses of course, and couldn't go to school. But we got our education in other ways, she and I. What a youth we had. Though her death so young was a tragedy, not every memory is sad."

Such stories were manna to Elspeth, starved as she was for any affectionate word of her parents. "I wish I could remember her. I will own I envy you her memories—even the sad ones."

"Oh, you are the loveliest of girls." Her aunt took her hand. "Just like her. And very much like him, too—made for happiness. He was always the most interesting man in any room—people were just attracted to him, like a polestar, because he delighted in the world as he found it. He rather gloried in the messiness of the human condition, in the sublime and the ridiculous. He liked it all, bless his heart. He liked to laugh, and he liked play, and he like to drink, but oh, how he loved. He loved freely. Generously."

"He loved my mother?"

"With all his heart. There was never anyone else for him ever—except you. And he loved you. Very, very much. Enough that he braved those two pecking old sparrows, the sisters Murray, to make sure that you would be safe and cared for in the end."

Elspeth mouth ran dry, but she asked the question that had been burning in the back of her tongue ever since the moment she had known of her new aunt's existence. "Why did he not leave me with you?"

It had haunted her of late, in the dark of the night—the possibility that this life of imagination and ease and light and laughter might have been hers sooner.

"Ah, my darling child." She took Elspeth's hand, but for

the first time, the mirth dimmed from her Aunt Augusta's eyes. "I have often wished he had, but the truth is, it mightn't have turned out so well had he done so. I was not married to my dear Admiral Ivers then, and I did not have this lovely house as a safe haven to give you."

There was a certain relief, mixed with a certain disappointment, that her lot in life was not the product of some awful mischance or unkind machination on the part of the Aunts. "I see."

"I hope you do. Your father did the right thing in taking you to the Murrays. I still think so, though I will admit that I never thought that they would keep you from me for all of these many long years. But"—her aunt took a deep, cleansing breath, as if to throw off such sorrowful thoughts—"I wonder what might have been, if he'd had more time on this earth, your father. If grief and the drink hadn't killed him. I wonder if that story in the trunk mightn't have been the making of him." Aunt Augusta shook her head and turned away, out the window, as if some fresh idea were worrying at her head. "And I wonder if it would be possible now…"

"If what would be possible, Aunt?"

"The book," she clarified vaguely. "I had been toying with an idea… I thought to revive his legacy—and if I'm to be honest, earn some money so you, his heir, might have some sort of independent fortune that the sisters Murray could not refuse, for they would never take any money from me."

"How thoughtful."

Aunt Augusta waved away any praise. "I thought a new version of the old book, cleaned up for present tastes, might be attempted. But what you said—about his writing making you want to make up stories of your own—I wonder if the same could be done with the pages in the trunk. It could be done, I suppose." She closed her eyes, as if she could picture it clearly, this new book. And the she opened them to look at Elspeth, as if seeing her anew. "By you, Elspeth."

"Me? Finish the story?"

"Yes, but make it a different sort of book—a less *picaresque* book."

Elspeth's heart began clattering like the old spinning wheel—everything within her was afraid and aghast and exhilarated all at the same time. "I don't know if I ought—"

"Oh, life is too short for doing only what one *ought*, my dear girl. Those pages are your father's legacy to you—they are your fortune in foolscap just waiting to be redeemed." Aunt Augusta sat back and took a long sip of tea. "Or not. However you choose, my dear girl."

Elspeth thought about the fragile pages that had sifted and rustled through her fingers, as if they were whispering for her attention. As if they had an answer to a question she had not yet asked. As if they might be the antidote to the years and years of cap-wearing spinsterhood that stretched in front of her like an endlessly muddy lane.

The idea began as the flicker of a flame in the back of her mind, warming slowly, coming gradually toward the light. Gathering heat. And purpose.

"I would just write down the stories I've already imagined?"

"Just so."

"And perhaps think of some more? To make them flow together?" There were some scenes amongst the pages of foolscap that just didn't fit with the others—as if her father had perhaps let his imagination run wild without a thought for the rest of the book. But she might let her imagination run a bit less wild and fill in the seeming gaps in the story.

"And why not?" Aunt Augusta laughed. "You may do just as you please."

Why not, indeed.

For the second time in her life, Elspeth decided to do just as she pleased.

Chapter 7

IT HAD TAKEN Herculean effort and nearly a month of persuasion, but thankfully, not all of his ready money, for Hamish to prevail upon old Abel Prufrock to make him a partner of Prufrock & Company. What Abel Prufrock lacked in vision, he made up for with experience, and Hamish was happy to supply all the vision in the world for a chance to revive the company's fortunes along with his own.

As soon as the ink was dry on the partnership agreement, Hamish turned his mind to implementing that vision. "What we need, Prufrock, are steady, sure things that are guaranteed to sell, and which we can publish in regular intervals—in small but profitable batches to keep the costs down—like the Otis book. No more of your slim volumes of poetry printed in only three presentation copies."

"But we're living in a great age for poetry, my lad," Prufrock objected.

"That's all well and good for art, dear sir, but poetry is not profitable. We have to think larger if we're to survive." And Hamish meant to do more than survive—he meant to thrive. He meant to increase his fortune as expeditiously as possible, so come Whitsunday, he could tell his father just what he could do with his talk of fillies and heirs and unsteadiness.

But first he had to revise the Otis book. And while he had

written his fair share of exceedingly indifferent poetry, he had never yet taken his hand to prose.

Hamish's attention was diverted from his problem by the sudden jangle of the bell over the door announcing the arrival of a wide-eyed female clutching a tight-wrapped parcel to her chest.

At a glance, she was exactly the sort of country mouse of a female—all modest, down-cast eyes peeping up from under a country cloak—who could be expected to offer them a slim volume of poetry to be printed in three presentation copies— one for herself, another for her grandmother, and the third for her cat. She'd be eaten up by Edinburgh's rats if she didn't mind herself.

But before he could shoo said female from the premises, she turned those wide, lethally innocent eyes upon Prufrock, who seemed to have little natural defense against predators of such a stealthy sort. "Mr. Prufrock?"

"Indeed, I am he." Prufrock rose as swiftly as his creaking knees would allow, bowing his rosy, polished head in her direction. "How might I be of service?"

"Good afternoon, sir." The lass nipped a wee dip of a curtsey. "I believe you to have been the publisher of—"

"If I may?" Hamish broke in before Prufrock could commit them to another money-sinking endeavor. "I take it you've a slim volume of sentimental but uplifting verse you should like to see published?" He smiled to ease the way to her disappointment. "Alas, Prufrock & Company are no longer in the market for poetry."

The mousie blinked at him. "But I haven't, sir. Got poetry, that is." She gestured with the parcel held across her chest. "I've a novel."

Hamish was not about to be diverted, even by the promise of a novel. Even by a novel offered with a wide-eyed, fetchingly fey smile. "A novel in three volumes, with a morally uplifting theme, and a worthy orphan for a protagonist?" The sort of tale meant to frighten young misses to keep quietly to their country mouse holes. "I'm afraid we're still not interested. Good day."

"Nay." The wee mousie bit down on her soft lower lip. "Although I'm not exactly sure what a *pro-tagonist* is, sir, but if it's the same as the h——"

Ye gods. Hamish held up his hand to stop her from saying another word. The sooner he got her out of there, the sooner he could return to the business at hand in reviving Prufrock & Company's prospects.

"As I was saying——" He stepped toward the door so he could hold it open for her to leave.

But she whisked herself away, deeper into the space, to hold her ground. "It is a romantic novel. A *very* romantic novel." She spoke quickly, in a rush to get the words out before he might stop her. "A new, very romantic novel by a man"—her voice grew firmer and more animated—"you published some years ago. Mr. John Otis."

The mention of such a name—the *very* name that had been on the tip of Hamish's tongue for weeks—brought even arthritic Prufrock around his desk. "New? By John Otis? Why, he's been dead these twenty years."

"The same John Otis who was the author of *A Memoir of a Game Girl?*" Hamish asked. The manuscript he was counting upon to make their fortune?

"Aye." The wee mousie nodded. "The same. It's a new manuscript, written some years ago, but only just come to light."

Prufrock leaned on the large, two-sided desk for support. "Well, I'll be."

They'd be rich, is what they'd be, if the lass's claim were true.

"A romantic story, you said?" Hamish asked. "How romantic?" John Otis's work had been, at best, characterized as amatory, but never romantic.

"*Highly* romantic," was her interesting answer.

Hamish pushed politeness aside to come straight to the point. "Erotic?"

The lass's boldness went up in a flush of color so hot, Hamish was afraid her green velvet hood might catch fire. "Somewhat less than...*that.*" She swallowed and tried to stand tall—well, as tall as a willowy sort of lass who looked as if a stiff wind might blow her down could. "I can only assume that with this particular manuscript, Mr. Otis sought to avoid the scandal and trouble that the last book occasioned. One can't sell a banned book, can one?"

It was so insightful an understatement, Hamish took a closer look at the wee slip of a lass. Under that country cloak were bright, clear blue eyes in a pointed, oval face. An intelligent face. A pretty face.

If one liked that curious country mouse sort. Which he didn't. Because he had a business to run, a fortune to make, and a wedding to avoid.

But he could put up with a country miss for the sake of a publishable book.

"Do come in." He swept her a more credible bow. "I take it you have this manuscript with you?"

"I have the first half of the volume," the lass confirmed. "I was leery of…letting the whole of it out of my hands without a firm contract. I thought to…gauge the level of interest before I did so."

"Very prudent," Prufrock assured her.

"Give it here," was Hamish's more mercenary demand. "And we'll see if there is anything worth giving a contract for." Hamish was already cutting open the wrapping before he thought to kick a chair in her direction. "Have a seat."

She did not sit—her glance flitted from the chair to the door, and then back at him, as if gauging how long she could bear to stay. "How long will you need to contemplate the pages?"

"No time a'tall." He made her nervous, which delighted and bothered him, all at the same time, though he couldn't tell why. But what he did know was that the pages looked well prepared, written in a clean, clear hand, which bothered *him*— the Otis manuscript in his possession was nothing so tidy. "If it really is by John Otis, as you say."

"It is," she assured him. But she bit her lip—more mousie and less confident now.

Hamish pressed his advantage. "And how did you come

by this remarkable find?"

But the mousie proved less pliable than she looked. "And you are?" She looked away from him, toward his partner. "I had thought I would be dealing with Mr. Prufrock, as the prior publisher of John Otis's book."

Prufrock made the belated introductions. "Mr. Cathcart is my business partner. The newest partner of Prufrock & Company."

"Oh, michty me!" The lass drew back as if she'd been scalded. "Cathcart like the earl? You're the earl's son? I beg your pardon, sir."

Hamish took notice of her careful re-appraisal of him, and reckoned she was just like everyone else—wondering if, because he was in trade, he was the illegitimate son.

He let her wonder. "And *you* are?"

"Miss Elspeth Otis," she finally supplied. "I'm John Otis's daughter."

Ye Gods.

Hamish sat before he could fall. Because, it seemed there was at least one illegitimate person in the room after all.

Chapter 8

ELSPETH HURRIED BACK to the house on St. Andrew Square in good time for afternoon tea. Aunt Augusta awaited her in the sunny, comfortable salon at the back of the house overlooking a blooming walled garden, with every appearance of ease, but Elspeth thought she could detect some anxiousness in her greeting. But perhaps that was her own anxiety coloring her perception.

"There you are, my dear. Come in, come in and take some refreshment after your adventure." She held out a welcoming hand to gather Elspeth to her side. "How did you find Mr. Prufrock? Did you conclude your business satisfactorily?"

Elspeth took a deep breath to ease the tangle of her conscience. "I found Mr. Prufrock amiable and quiet, but it was his partner, a Mr. Cathcart, who conducted the greater share of the business."

"Ah." Aunt Augusta paused as if she were not sure how she liked such an event. "And how did you find Mr. Cathcart?"

"Less amiable." Elspeth's first impression of Mr. Cathcart had not been entirely favorable—he seemed to be just the sort of man her Aunts Murray had always warned her about—far too handsome, and far too sure of himself for Elspeth's comfort. But again—her impression had been colored by her own anxiety. "I have a confession to make."

"Gracious. What about?"

"I lied—I told them that the book was written by my father—without telling them that I helped."

"Ah." Aunt Augusta was not nearly so shocked at this sign of Elpseth's perfidy. "Perhaps that is all for the better. Frankly, I should think it matters less who wrote it than if it is a wonderful book. And it is, Elspeth. You may be assured of that."

"But what if he can tell the difference? Mr. Cathcart was reading the manuscript pages when I left, for I could not bear to sit and watch him do so."

"Fret not, my love." The smile spread upwards to the corners of Aunt Augusta's eyes. "Mr. Cathcart has a reputation as a man with an acute eye as well as an astute man of business. I should think it will not be long before he has an answer—"

Aunt Augusta was interrupted by the sharp rap of the door knocker below. A pleased smile curved across her cheeks. "Just as I was saying—it won't be long at all. Your Mr. Cathcart is a pleasingly decisive young man."

"How can you know it is he at the door?" No name had been announced. "And he's certainly not *my* Mr. Cathcart."

"All in good time." Aunt Augusta favored her with a kindly, critical eye. "Take off your old cloak and sit here"— she gestured to a watered silk-upholstered chair—"with your back to the window. It will put you in just the right light."

"The right light for what?"

"For Mr. Cathcart's astute eye." Augusta hurried to take her own seat opposite as the butler, Reeves, announced their visitor.

"Mr. Hamish Cathcart, my lady."

"Ah." Aunt Augusta's satisfaction at being proved right was all cat-in-cream pleasure. "Do show him in, Reeves."

Mr. Cathcart came into the room like a gust of fresh spring air, all bracing bonhomie. "My dear Lady Ivers." He bowed low over Aunt Augusta's hand. "How good of you to see me."

In the brighter light of the salon, Elspeth could see more

clearly what she had nervously tried to dismiss in the dimmer confines of Fowl's Close—Mr. Cathcart was a tall, extraordinarily well-formed, exceptionally handsome fellow. Even if he did smile a bit too easily. Especially since he was now turning the force of that smile upon her.

"And Miss Otis. A pleasure to see you again." He approached her just as he had Aunt Augusta, and bowed over her hand. But he looked up at her just before he placed a kiss upon the curve of her wrist.

And just like that, Elspeth felt upended, as if her brain had gone topsy-turvy and upside-down.

It was exactly as the Aunts Murray had always warned—she would find her head turned, and there would be nothing she could do about it if she were not always vigilant. Elspeth had been extremely vigilant, but she was dazzled despite the warnings, and even as she scolded herself not to be.

But she was home now, with her Aunt Augusta who knew all and forgave all, and there was no need to feel as nervous as a guinea fowl in a fox's den. She was four and twenty after all—her advanced age ought to provide her with some protection against such provocative charm.

And if not, Aunt Augusta, was vixen enough to deal with Mr. Cathcart.

"Ah." Aunt Augusta said for the third time, investing that single word with a wealth of meaning—most importantly that she was thoroughly in control. "Hamish. You've already met my dear niece, Miss Otis, but a short while ago. And here you are. How fascinating. I was just asking my niece how she found you."

He laughed. "Forward, I should think."

"Well, you certainly aren't backward." The tart retort was out of Elspeth's mouth before she could think. But she would not regret it, for he had not been invited, and Elspeth had certainly not given him her aunt's direction. Indeed, she had never once even mentioned her aunt's name.

But things at her Aunt Augusta's house in the city seemed to be a great deal less formal or fussy than they had been under the stricter eyes of the sisters Murray. Here, things were a great deal less *comme il faut* than they were come-as-you-are.

Here, Aunt Augusta laughed and agreed with both of them. "Yes, indeed, Hamish, for you are not backward in the least. How clever you are to come straightaway."

"You are too kind, my lady." Mr. Cathcart took the chair opposite and was already leaning forward, focusing his gaze on Elspeth with a sort of sharp attention that made her decidedly uncomfortable. "What both you and Miss Otis will now find me is enthusiastic."

"Just as I said—clever. How did you know my niece would be here, with me?"

He favored Aunt Augusta with what the Aunts Murray might have characterized as a roguish grin—no hint of apology. "I set an apprentice to follow your carriage, naturally."

"So, you think it's good?"

"You would not have sent her to me, and I should not be here were it not."

"Excellent." Aunt Augusta clapped her hands, and reached to take Elspeth's cold fingers between her own. "It's just as I told you, Elspeth—it is a wonderful book that—"

"—that could not have been written by John Otis," Mr. Cathcart finished. "At least not in its entirety." He turned the lethal charm of his focus upon Elspeth once more. "Tell me, Miss Otis, how long did it take you to prepare the manuscript? I noticed the copy you gave me was in your hand and not your father's script."

Wariness landed like cold porridge in the pit of her stomach. "Yes, well, it took several weeks to…transcribe the story from the crumbling foolscap he had written it upon." The Aunts would castigate her for her sloppy grammar. "Upon which he wrote. And I must admit, some parts, you see, needed to be invented fresh—to fill in the…gaps."

Mr. Cathcart appeared to care nothing for her grammar. Or her prevarication. "Excellent. Very timely work. And did you find it difficult or time-consuming, replacing all the naughty—or shall we be frank and call them erotic?—bits before you brought it to me?"

Elspeth felt her cheeks heat. What an astonishingly direct fellow he was—he said the word so matter-of-factly. Elspeth struggled to achieve the same level of sanguinity. "Well, not exactly difficult." It had actually been easy to substitute her own decidedly less carnal imaginings for the naughtier bits.

But Mr. Cathcart was having none of her havering. "Come, I beg you would be frank with me, Miss Otis." He smiled and leaned his head closer to chat amiably, as if they were alone, and she were already in his confidence. "I've seen John Otis's original writing—we have the original manuscript for *A Memoir of a Game Girl* at Prufrock's, you know. I can tell the difference."

"No, indeed, I am not bamming you, Mr. Cathcart—" Elspeth flicked a glance at Aunt Augusta, looking for some direction, but that lady only answered with her silent, feline smile—Elspeth was on her own.

So she racked her brain for some suitable explanation that would not be an outright lie, but would also not give away the whole of the game. "Well, you see—"

But it was as if Mr. Cathcart could see right through her fumbles—he chuckled and raised his eyebrows in tease. "You certainly are attempting to bam me. While I do understand your hesitation to reveal yourself to the world until you are assured of how the novel will be taken, I am as high as the moon over Auld Reeky to find you not just a purveyor of Otis's work, but a creative force in your own right."

Creative force. In her own right.

The words were like rays of light penetrating the wet weather of her former life—full of warm welcome she didn't want to refuse. But the habits of a lifetime could not be broken in the slim month she had been in the city. "Well, I am not exact—"

"Then who is?" He sat back and regarded her with suspicious smile. "As Prufrock said, John Otis has been dead and gone these twenty years. And what's more, the story you brought me is most assuredly not entirely from his pen. And I should know. I've been taking a long look at the story of Fanny Bahoochie with the idea of shaping Otis's words into something more commercially palatable—a form they do not naturally take, as I'm sure you're aware. The manuscript you offered me was more than palatable. It was genius."

Genius.

Something pleasing and not entirely manageable began to curl up in her chest, like a barn cat in a sunbeam. Pride—that was what her aunts, the sisters Murray, would name it, and take her to task. "You needn't try to flatter me—"

"Why not? I *should* flatter you, and rightly so. The book you've given me—the half of the book, and I shall want the other half straightaway—is damn fine, Miss Otis. Damn fine. I want to put it into production immediately. It matters not in the least to me that you, and not John Otis, really wrote it. In fact, it's better."

"Really? Better how?" She blinked at him, not understanding how such a thing could be possible. "John Otis is already famous—even if he is also rather infamous—and so will garner more attention if his name is upon the work."

"Indeed." He clapped his hands together in pleasure. "How clever of you to understand that, Miss Otis."

"So you do mean to publish it under his name?"

"I do." He extended his hand to shake in firm agreement. "I do intend to publish your book. And any more you might see fit to 'find'."

It hit her then—like a butt from a lamb, soft but insistent—the enormity of just what he was saying. He liked *her* book. He wanted *more*.

"Really? And truly? You're not just trying to butter up my parsnips?"

This time he laughed. "Really and truly. I will stake my last groat that not only will this book make your fortune as well as mine, but the next one will double it."

"Truly? A fortune? And the *next one*?"

"I have plans for you, Miss Elspeth Otis. May I call you Elspeth? And you must call me Hamish"—he went on without waiting for her reply—"for I feel we're bound to become the very closest of friends."

Chapter 9

THE TRUTH WAS, Hamish wanted to be more than friends.

How much more, he wasn't quite sure.

What was sure was that Miss Elspeth Otis was the rare sort of young woman he actually liked—imaginative and intelligent, and ambitious for something other than a husband. A lass who didn't mind using her mind. And what a mind. Illegitimate she might be, the fruit of the devil's own loins—for stories of John Otis' roisterous ways lived large in Edinburgh's collective memory—but by God, she could write like an angel.

In fact, Hamish liked her all the more for being illegitimate—she wasn't likely to be the kind of lass who would question an earl's son's involvement in business, or turn up her nose at his own family's decidedly irregular lineage. She was the perfect partner for him in all ways— clever as the day was long, disguising herself as a country mouse, when she was clearly no such thing—when her writing clearly told him she was blessedly experienced.

Hamish had never understood the virtues of ignorance, the absurd insistence on innocence in females—he'd never felt its attraction. Give him an honestly experienced lass who knew her own mind, and wasn't afraid of what people would say any day.

Aye, Elspeth Otis was perfect. In more ways than one— there were also those clear-sighted blue eyes, and those long, striding-about-the-countryside strong legs.

The manuscript she had brought him was as perfect as she—perfectly balanced between emotion and action. Perfectly calibrated toward a high romantic sensibility. And perfectly poised to make him a fortune.

But he would have bet his left nut if John Otis had actually written it. John Otis had been bawdy and inventive and told a romping good tale, but he never wrote anything so lyrical and sweepingly romantic that it nearly made a man want to abandon his footloose, unsteady ways and make an honest man of himself.

Nearly. Unsteady Hamish might be, but not unhinged.

Still, while he was taking advantage of Elspeth Otis's fine mind, there was no reason he might not also enjoy her fine looks. Without the cover of the old cloak, her wheat-blond hair shimmered in the pool of sunlight streaming through the window, and her delicate face was pink with pleasure. This afternoon, Miss Elspeth Otis was no wee gray mousie—she was a soft, sweet cygnet who had, in the time it had taken him to read enough to make his decision, turned into a poised, serene swan.

She was a clever one, his Miss Otis. Because somewhere beneath that calm surface lurked a delightfully naughty, extremely clever mind. And, oh, how he liked the clever ones.

And if he had his way—and he had learnt enough of charm to ensure that he nearly always did get his way—she'd like him just as well. And he already had her aunt, Lady Augusta Ivers' approval—in fact, she had all but hand-picked him for the part, hadn't she?

"Michty me." The lass shook her head again, as if she wasn't yet ready to accept the truth of his compliments, but pleasure began to shine in her lovely blue eyes. "It's all so overwhelming. It's as if it's too good to be true."

"Then I must convince you I am everything sincere. Because I have a proposition for you."

Color swept up her long, pale swan's neck and across her cheeks like a sunrise.

"A business proposition," he clarified. Although now that she looked so fetchingly flushed, he began to wonder what it might be like to follow that swath of heightened color beneath the modest cover of her linen fichu, all the way to the very edge of her bodice and beyond. Down beneath the confinement of her stays, where he would tug the last defense of her chemise down to reveal the sweet pink tip—

"You see"—Lady Ivers's enthusiastic, and correct, assumption brought him out of his dangerous daydream of Miss Otis's flushed flesh, and back to the business at hand— "Hamish had been thinking of revising *A Memoir of a Game Girl,* much as you've done so magnificently well with those old fragments of your father's."

"Aye." Hamish cleared his throat. "That I am. And what I've read of the manuscript you brought me is exactly what I want for the new edition of that novel."

"You mean you want *me*—" The lass's plum soft mouth fell open in astonishment. "To do it all again, with a second book?"

Hamish was nearly as gratified at having been right about Elspeth Otis's revision of the manuscript as he was excited at taking one step closer to that fortune just waiting to be made. "Indeed, I do. And I will contract with you for any further manuscripts you should care to 'find' or write after that. In fact, I predict any book written in the same style will be a pure, smashing success."

Elspeth gaped at him. "You're mad." But he could see the excitement—the lure of the possibilities—shining through her bright blue eyes.

"If I am, it's a fine madness. But I am perfectly in my right mind, and I know exactly what I am doing—offering you the princely sum of two hundred and fifty pounds." Hamish named the largest sum he thought he could reasonably afford without endangering their success and then added a little more—just to be sure. Prufrock & Company's reserves were only slightly more than three hundred, but the extra fifty pounds were his insurance against the competition snatching her up—there were plenty of publishing houses in Edinburgh who would know a good thing when they saw it. Best to sew the business up right and tight now.

"Two hundred…" Her voice faded—from outrage or astonishment, he could not tell.

For half a moment, Hamish wondered if he would have to offer more—how, he knew not. He had used up nearly all his available blunt to buy his half of the business.

Flustered Miss Elspeth Otis might have been, but she was no witless gudgeon. "Guineas?"

"Ye gods, nay! Do you think I am some lordling with more money than sense? I can't afford to pay you in gold." But he also couldn't afford to lose her. "Pounds sterling. But there's more to be made, I promise. I don't aim to cheat you, Elspeth Otis—your aunt will, I hope, vouchsafe my honesty and integrity."

"I will," Lady Ivers averred.

"There. Be assured I aim to make us both quite, quite rich."

"Quite, quite rich," Elspeth repeated, as if she were testing the idea of richness like the taste of chocolate torte on her tongue—a slow smile of incredulous wonder blossomed across her face. "Then, with my aunt's permission"—a nod sufficed to grant it—"I think the answer to your offer, Mr. Cathcart, is most certainly yes."

Hamish had never in his life felt such profound relief and pleasure all at the same time—he felt buoyed up, as if he were swimming in delight. "You, Elspeth Otis, are a treasure."

And to give exercise to the hot press of happiness, he picked her up as if she were made of feathers and fairy wings instead of experience and determination, and twirled them both around. And kissed her for good measure.

The moment his lips touched hers, what had been an instinctively hearty, heartfelt kiss of joy and relief and excitement threatened to turn into something altogether different. Altogether more personal.

And altogether too intimate.

"Ye gods." He was almost as astonished as poor Elspeth—he only stood dazed and confused, while he realized the enormity—the absolute disaster—of his mistake. She stood still with shock, her hands flown up to cover her mouth and cheeks. Experience aside, he had kissed her without any warning or permission, in broad daylight only a few hours after he had met her. And in front of her aunt.

Both of them looked at Lady Ivers, who mercifully said nothing, but waited with one raised brow for him to correct his mistake. Which he did immediately. "You must forgive me my thoughtless exuberance, Miss Otis. Lady Ivers, my apologies. I meant nothing disrespectful toward your niece. I was only—"

"Caught up in the moment?" the lady suggested kindly, though she did move strategically between them. "Yes, I can see. Gracious, but I hadn't counted on you being such a susceptible numpty, Hamish Cathcart, but I suppose you're only human after all."

Her patiently exasperated tone seemed to be just the thing—a sort of silly, slightly embarrassed amusement descended upon them like a light summer sun shower, lightening the moment.

Hamish could feel his face stretch into a rather stupid grin, and even poor Elspeth's lips began to curve into a shy smile. He tucked his chin and gave her his most charmingly susceptible smile. "Forgive me?"

Her embarrassment was overtaken by the charm of the moment. "I suppose I must," she said on a breathless little smile.

"You must," he insisted, taking her hand. "For I've already written to several booksellers in London, as well as Glasgow, Manchester, Liverpool and Leeds. We're going to print as many copies as we can afford, and then stand ready to print more. We'll have the two books out one after the other, each feeding the demand for the other." The thought was another buoy to his spirits. "Much as it pains me to predict it, I expect you'll also be buried under invitations and bombarded with posies. Prepare yourself, my dear Miss Otis, to be all the rage."

Chapter 10

"REALLY?" ELSPETH HAD never been *anything*, much less something as exciting as a rage. "Do you really think the book will do that well?"

"Not just the book. But you, Miss Elspeth Otis."

Elspeth had never been so full of excitement and misgivings all at the same time, wanting to believe him—to believe in the possibilities—but having so little experience in doing so.

"Come, my darlings." Aunt Augusta clapped her hands. "We must celebrate such an auspicious new beginning. Tell me you like champagne, Hamish."

"Certainly, my lady," Mr. Cathcart demurred with an easy smile. "If you will forgive me being out of evening clothes to drink it."

"I will readily forgive you. We are not so high in the instep as to put off a celebration on such paltry grounds. Elspeth, ring for Reeves, if you'd be so kind, and tell him we'll have a bottle of champagne from my dear friend *Monsieur* Clicquot."

"Of course." The bell was duly rung, and the bottle duly brought.

Elspeth had, in the month since her arrival, tasted wine with her suppers, but she had never tasted anything like the ticklish confection that budded on the tip of her tongue and made delight bubble into her veins. "Michty me, that's marvelous!"

"A toast to your collaboration." Aunt Augusta raised her glass. "To your success."

"To success," said Mr. Cathcart.

"Oh, yes, success," Elspeth agreed. It was all so remarkable—this life she seemed to be leading, which she could not even have imagined a month earlier in her attic bedroom in Twelve Mile Burn. She was an author—she had best think like one. "How long is this other book that you want me to..."—she searched for the appropriate word for 'taking the naughty bits out.'

"Rewrite? Yes, the length will be a challenge—the *Memoir of a Game Girl* is nearly three-hundred pages long, and excessively amatory, as I'm sure you'll recall."

Elspeth did not, in fact, recall, as the sisters Murray had never allowed her to read any novel, much less an excessively amatory one penned by *that Wastrel.* She would have to hope that Aunt Augusta had a copy that she could read when Mr. Cathcart was not there, smiling down at her with that happy, encouraging, thoroughly expectant grin.

"I don't mind telling you how pleased I am that I convinced you to take on the job, as it were," he said. "I didn't have the faintest idea how to go about it myself."

Elspeth was giddy enough to give him the truth. "Well, I suppose I'll just go about it the same as I did the first time— one careful, prudent snip at a time, like the overgrown honeysuckle vine in the garden, pruning away the deadwood to cultivate new growth."

He laughed. "And there is both the perfect metaphor, and an example of the rustic charm you put into that manuscript. It's brilliant."

Brilliant. The word went to her head as effortlessly as the champagne. "Well," she confessed. "I just thought of the book I'd like to read, and wrote that instead."

"Full of romance and yearning?" he laughed to show what he thought of romance and yearning. "But you're too clever to believe all that."

Her giddiness was momentarily tempered by a disorienting feeling of apprehension—Elspeth was not sure if she had been damned with faint praise, or simply disparaged. But she did not want to be thought a fool. "I suppose."

"Well, whatever it is," he went on, "it makes good reading. And hopefully good money."

"Thank you, Mr. Cathcart. Yes," Elspeth replied now that she understood romantic yearnings were acceptable only in the pursuit of commerce. "I hope so, too."

"Now, I thought we'd agreed not to be so formal—you must call me Hamish, as your aunt does."

"Thank you. And you must call me Elspeth."

"I should be honored, Elspeth." He clasped her hand as if she were a man, pumping it as exuberantly as if she were a sportsman whose horse had won a race. "I meant what I said. I should very much like to be your friend."

Until that moment, Elspeth had thought she would like nothing more than to have the friendship of such a clever and handsome man. But the moment her hand was enveloped in his, she felt differently—warmed from the inside despite the chill his cynical words had given her.

Or perhaps the warmth was all his, and the cynicism hers? Perhaps she had listened for too long to her Aunts Murray's warnings against the laxity lying in wait in her blood, and her dangerous susceptibility to worthless pleasures?

But why should she not have at least some pleasure? Why should she not enjoy the exuberant attraction of a clever, handsome man?

"Did you really mean it when you said you should like any other manuscripts I might have?"

His face lit like a Guy Fawkes Night bonfire, full of burning interest. "Have you any more?"

"Well, not like my father's books, and not at the present time written down, but I've stories." All the stories she had made up to occupy her hours over the years. All the characters she had created to keep her company through the solitary country hours. All the wonderfully wild imaginings that had formed her vision of the world. "Although most of them are not at all *excessively amatory*"—thanks to the champagne, the words winged off her tongue without the least hesitation or embarrassment—"but just as full of rustic charm."

"And romantic yearning?" His voice was as teasing as his smile.

Which suddenly gave her pause. Gracious, was Mr. Cathcart actually *flirting* with her?

Elspeth had so little experience with the practice, she wasn't sure—the only person to ever speak to her at all warmly had been the son of the vicar of Twelve Mile Burn's kirk, St. Kentigerna the Recluse, and the Aunts Murray had somehow seen to it that the lad was shipped off to school somewhere, never to return to their village.

"Perhaps less of that, as well." Elspeth gathered her giddy courage. "I mostly make up stories about the animals."

Mr. Cathcart's look might best be described as dumbfounded—as if he could not conceive of how such a story might be in any way interesting. Or publishable.

"I treat them like people, you see—the rabbits and voles, and hedgehogs and badgers. They are the *protagonists*." She used his own word to show him she had been listening. "I used to draw them, too, when I had time. But paper was dear and watercolors terrible expensive."

"Do you meant like that darling little sketch you made of the housekeeper's cat?" Aunt Augusta interposed. "The one with the two mischievous mice on the shelf above?"

"Aye. Not that there are mice in your kitchen larder, I'm sure," she hastened to assure Aunt Augusta, "but the cat was looking so complacent, I just thought—"

"You just *imagined*," Aunt Augusta finished for her. "Oh, you are your parents' child—both of them—equal parts talent and whimsy. Well, I shall purchase you papers and paints first thing on the morrow, so you will have them to give you pleasure if nothing else, but also so you can show Hamish what you are talking about."

It was all so easy with Aunt Augusta—there was never an

impediment that could not be overcome. "Thank you, dear aunt. I don't know how I shall ever repay you."

Aunt Augutsa raised her glass. "By being happy, dear Elspeth. By simply being happy."

"Here, here." Hamish Cathcart raised his glass as well. "And I look forward to whatever story of whatever sort you should like to write."

"Thank you." Elspeth drained her own glass. She felt as light as air and twice as happy. If she had had the paper and colors Aunt Augusta promised to hand, she would have sat right down to indulge her imagination right there on the spot so she might show her aunt more of the creatures peopling her daydreams. And show Hamish Cathcart, too.

But Aunt Augusta was taking charge of the conversation, "Now tell me, Hamish, what are your plans for our dear Elspeth? Don't think I'm going to let you work her to death like an apprentice. She has already sacrificed far too much time in the service of your precious manuscripts when she could have been out and about in society."

"But the book is precious to me, too, Aunt Augusta." Elspeth wanted that made clear. "I should very much like to earn an independence from my legacy from my father."

Her aunt agreed. "And of course, you will earn a very handsome independence—I shall make sure that you do. Indeed, Hamish will supply us with his contracts, and I shall have my man of business go over them with you, so you will know your interests are being protected."

"Thank you, Aunt Augusta." Elspeth reached for her glass—which had miraculously been refilled with champagne—and raised it to her aunt. "I should like that. I've had a small taste of Mr. Cathcart's bargaining in Fowl's Close, and I should very much like to even up the score a bit."

Both Aunt Augusta and Hamish Cathcart laughed, and Mr. Cathcart answered. "You had me fooled in Fowl's Close, for I should never have taken you for a pirate, Miss Elspeth Otis."

"There are no pirate ships amongst the hedgerows in Twelve Mile Burn, Mr. Cathcart."

"Hamish," he corrected. "But I should have known your were a pirate from the way you batted your lashes at poor Abel Prufrock as if they were scatterguns."

Now he was accusing her of flirting! "I never. But you'd know a thing or two of piracy, wouldn't you, Hamish Cathcart, snapping your fingers"—she mimicked his action, and lowered her voice to approximate his baritone—"'Give it here. I'll see if there is anything worth giving two scatterguns for.'"

He laughed. "And now I am sure that we will get along absolutely famously."

"I was sure you would." Aunt Augusta smiled at them both. "For you each have what the other lacks."

"I lack Miss Otis's brilliance."

Elspeth could not help but smile. "And I lack your printing press."

"A partnership made in heaven," Aunt Augusta opined.

"Indeed. And I thank you as well, Lady Ivers," Hamish Cathcart inclined his head to his host. "For being the impetus for this entire endeavor—I have not forgotten that it was you who put Prufrock in my sights. I have never had such a good prospect given to me so easily, and at such little cost."

"Oh, you'll pay your debt to me yet, Hamish," the lady said into her champagne glass, so that Elsepth only heard the happy murmur. "You may feel free to stop by any time to converse with Elspeth on business matters. I am sure you will need to work on producing her book right away, while she works on her father's."

"I will do so, with your permission. In fact, I should like to call tomorrow—at your earliest convenience, Miss Otis— to bring those contracts you requested, and to start to work on the second manuscript."

"No time like the present?"

"And needs must while the devil drives," he answered Aunt Augusta with a laugh. "I confess I like to work with the heat of a project in me. I hope you won't mind."

"Not at all." Elspeth was happy of any reason to see him again. She should like nothing better than to spend the next day—and the next—with him if he would keep smiling at her like that.

Aunt Augusta rose to signal the end of the small celebration. "As much as I should like to linger, I will plead your pardon and retire. Elspeth, darling, do be a dear and see Hamish out."

All by herself? But Aunt Augusta was not nearly the stickler for the proprieties that the Aunts Murray had been—she simply breezed out of the room, leaving Elspeth quite alone with Hamish Cathcart with nothing but her own good sense to guard against impropriety.

And her own good sense was a great deal muzzied by champagne.

As perhaps was his—the moment Aunt Augusta was gone from the dining room Hamish Cathcart reached for Elspeth's hand. "I'm already looking forward to tomorrow." He squeezed her fingers as if he could impress his sincerity and exuberance upon her. "I can't wait to get started."

He rose with his fingers still entwined with hers, and so she rose, too.

And of a sudden he was so close and so tall and so near she had to tip her head back to look up into this laughing brown eyes, crinkled up at the corners with what she was coming to recognize as exuberant glee.

"Isn't it marvelous? I have a feeling about this—don't you?" He asked before he seemed to answer his own question. "Don't you feel it, too?"

And then his hands were on her shoulders and around her back, drawing her close, holding her tight against his chest as his mouth covered hers.

She was being kissed—he was kissing her.

She could hardly think and barely breathe—his lips covered hers as if he was not yet close enough and needed to be closer still. He slanted his head—or was it hers?—to make them fit together just so.

Just so he could fan one hand along her jaw and cradle her head with the other. Just so she could slide her arms around his waist and hold him tight as his tongue found hers and began a dance so dizzying she thought she might fall down.

But she didn't—she was buoyed up by his words. "You taste like champagne," he whispered against her ear. "All bubbles and stars."

She felt as if bubbles and stars were flowing in her veins. She felt everything—the firm smoothness of his lips, the rough scratch of his whiskers beneath the surface of his skin, the heady tang of claret upon his tongue. "You taste like more, please."

She had no idea why she said it, but it was true—she wanted more of him. More of his warmth, more of his strength, more of his surety.

And much more of his lips pressed to hers.

It was as if four and twenty years of waiting and wanting and longing were at last distilled down to this moment of pleasure. She didn't want it to end.

But Hamish was taking her firmly by the shoulders to stand her away—to put distance between them. But still he smiled. "I shouldn't have done that," he admitted. "But damned if I'm not glad I did."

"So am I."

He laughed and pressed one more kiss to her lips, and stepped away. And bowed.

And left her alone, floating upon air.

Chapter 11

IN THE MORNING, Elspeth's head rang like an empty coal scuttle—all ashy and clanking.

"Too much champagne, darling?" Aunt Augusta asked not unkindly as she passed her a cup of blessedly hot morning chocolate.

"Do you think so?" Elspeth whispered, for anything louder hurt her brain something fierce.

"Oh, I know so, darling. Drink up your chocolate and have something to eat. And if that doesn't make you feel better, take a headache powder. For your Mr. Cathcart will be here sooner rather than later, if I'm any judge. And I am." She smiled over her teacup. "So prepare yourself for another onslaught of charm."

"Is that what it was last night—just charm?"

"Charm and a good deal more, my darling." Aunt Augusta turned her head at the sound of the knocker being applied with far too much force. "Now there he is. Take that toast, it will do you the world of good."

She breezed out of the room again, and in the time it took Elspeth to chomp down a jam covered slice of toast, reappeared with Hamish Cathcart in tow.

"Elspeth," he greeted her with his characteristic enthusiasm, and a roguish lack of consciousness. Just as if he hadn't been kissing her silly the last time they spoke.

As if she wasn't at that very moment reliving the moment—she could feel her cheeks heat red.

"And here is my man of business, Mr. Smythe, on your heels. Exactly on time, as always. Good morning Mr. Smythe. We'll sit here, whilst we go over these contracts " She indicated the arm chairs nearer to the hearth with one hand, while she held out her empty palm for Hamish to fill with his contracts. "The young people may take the table, to work on their own papers."

"Indeed, my lady." He bowed in obeisance, and then Hamish Cathcart turned the full force of that smiling regard upon Elspeth. "Good morning, Elspeth." His voice was low and laced with familiarity.

The warmth of his enthusiasm dispelled her headache faster than any powder. As did the sure span of his hand against the small of her back as he helped her to her seat. As did the way her drew his chair up close so his knees bumped against hers beneath the table.

"Good morning, Hamish," she answered, not caring that she sounded quite out of breath.

His smile climbed up to crinkle the corner of his eyes before he attempted to get to the business at hand. He set down a thick, typeset manuscript. "I suppose we ought to get to work."

"I suppose we had better," she answered, schooling her own smile into something that would not excite Aunt Augusta's interest. But a glance showed that lady quite rapt in her dry discussion of contracts with Mr. Smythe.

"Well then." Hamish cleared his throat as if he were realigning his thinking to more businesslike matters. "I thought it easiest to give you an old proof to work from." He shifted the stack of paper in front of her. "After the masterful job you made of the found manuscript, I've no doubt you can make something romantically sweet and yearning out of all this carnal desire."

"Michty me." And just like that, any good sense that had survived both the champagne and the headache fled, to be replaced by an exquisite awareness of Hamish Cathcart as a man—a man who, no doubt, had his own carnal desires. Desires she had only ever imagined.

He laughed, as if her oath was meant to be amusing. "Our job—and by our, I mean *your* job—is to transform young Fanny's sexual awakening and adventures into something more sweepingly romantic. For such things exist more easily in a book, I'll warrant, than they do in true life."

Elspeth hardly knew where to look, much less what to say. Not even a month in Aunt Augusta's cosmopolitan household could prepare her for such a speech. His practical cynicism entirely damped her native—and she now recognized, *naïve*—optimism. 'Carnal desire' had been bad enough, but 'sexual awakening' was so far beyond her experience, that she could only sit there, steaming like a Christmas pudding in her own embarrassment.

But he seemed not to notice. "When was the last time you read your father's book?" he asked.

She had nothing in her—no euphemism, no worldliness—but the truth. "Never," she whispered over the heat parching her throat. "I was never allowed."

"Never allowed?" Hamish sat back in surprise, and glanced at her aunt where she conferred by the hearth. "I would have thought Lady Ivers more a woman of the world than to forbid you books."

"Nay, not Lady Ivers." Elspeth swallowed her mortification like one of Aunt Molly's bitter nostrums—best gotten down quickly. It was past time for the whole of the truth. "It was not she, but my other kin, my mother's family, with whom I've lived all my life—I came to Edinburgh but lately from a village to the southwest." She gestured vaguely in the direction of the Borders. "They, those relations, thought…little of my father's book. And less of my father."

The frown etched itself into a single line pleating his brow lifted. "The country cloak," he said as if that answered for everything. "It did occur to me to wonder why I had ne'er met you before." He shook his head, as if realigning his thinking, and then looked at her again—peered, really—in that minutely assessing way that made heat scorch up the back of her neck and spread under her skin. "At first glance I did take you entirely for a country girl."

Elspeth had to clear her throat to find her voice, though it was still little more than a whisper. "The plain fact of the matter, Mr. Cathcart, is that I am almost entirely a country girl." For the past month had taught her a great deal, it could not change who she was deep down—nothing but a naïve dreamer. "And I know little of…awakenings."

"Ye gods." There was a long, awful moment of blistering silence while he sat up straight, and considered her anew, as if she were some unexpectedly thorny plant in a vegetable garden. "Then how did you re-write the first book?"

"As I told you last night—" At least she thought she had told him last night—the champagne made it hard to remember. "My theory was to go at it bit by bit, like pruning a rose bush—very carefully and with very sharp shears."

"But how did you come up with the new bits?" He lowered his own voice to a conspiratorial murmur. "All that sweeping romance?"

She had to wet her lips to get them to talk. "I just imagined it, I suppose."

"You just imagined it?" he repeated, as if he did not believe her. As if he could not contemplate such a thing. "Don't tell me you imagined it was hedgehogs?"

She looked up at him, but saw no disdain in his eyes, only gentle teasing. "I'll have you know the hedgehogs are hopeless romantics, believing someone will love them despite all those prickly spines. But it is the badgers who love with the most unrequited ardor. Quite deeply steadfast, the badgers."

"Oh, Elspeth." He took her hand between his, and drew it safely beneath the table. "So it was all flights of fancy? All *theory*? You've never—?"

His question was so sympathetic, she spared no thought for prevarication. "No," she said simply. There was nothing else she could say.

"And may I ask"—his voice went so low and quiet she

had to lean toward him to hear—"if I may be so bold, whether last night was perchance your first kiss?"

Elspeth felt her face flame so hot she might have cooked horse chestnuts on her cheeks. Her voice was the barest shred of admission. "It was."

"Ye gods." He passed a hand over his eyes as if the thought pained him. "Then you must forgive me. What a bungle I made of the job."

Elspeth's mortification returned in a rush that drained her cheeks of heat. "Kissing me was a *job*, was it?"

"Nay," he answered on a swift, self-mocking laugh, reaching for her hand again. "Not at all. Not if done right. And I was an ass for not getting it right. For assuming—" He rubbed his jaw with his free hand as if he might scrub his assumptions right out of his head. "I apologize. But I don't regret it. I enjoyed kissing you too much for regret."

"Oh. Good." His declaration warmed her more than she supposed it ought. But there was the truth of it—she didn't regret kissing him either. "Thank you."

His smile spread slowly across his face. "You are being very sweet and very polite, but I think you must have been astonished at my forwardness—or perhaps not, since you had already found me forward when we met."

"Aye, I suppose I had." She could feel her own smile return along with her equanimity—if he could laugh at himself, so could she.

"Well, it's the truth," he admitted. "I am forward." He bent his head closer to impart his confidence. "And I would be more forward still, were it not for that lady sitting not ten feet from us."

Elspeth cast a quick glance at Aunt Augusta in close conversation with her Mr. Smythe, and it seemed Hamish Cathcart came closer still, for his words seemed to whisper in her ear.

"If she were not there, I'd offer right here and now to give you a proper introduction to kissing. Lessons even."

This was not flirting but charm—this extraordinary ability to amuse and entice and banish her fears all at the same time.

"Lessons in kissing?" She looked up at him. "Do you think I need them?"

He shook his head, and clasped her hand in reassurance. "Nay. But that is neither here nor there, dear Elspeth. The question is whether you think you might *like* a lesson in kissing? And if you might like to give me a second chance at that first kiss?"

And there was her bad blood heating to make her heart sing like a morning lark at his offer. "I didn't think there was anything wrong with the first kiss."

He closed his eyes, even as he smiled. "You're going to kill me, Elspeth Otis, sitting there so sweetly. Saying such sweetly provocative things."

"You are teasing me, Mr. Cathcart." She grew surer of it even as she spoke. "This"—she pointed to the stacked proof pages of her father's book—"is provocative—I am merely provincial. But I think I may be learning something of awakenings after all."

He sat back as if the wind had been knocked right out of him. "Hamish," he finally said. "Do please call me Hamish if you're having an…awakening."

"Hamish, then."

"Ye gods, Elspeth." That roguish smile began to reclaim its pride of place on his face. "Do you know, I think I have approached this all wrong."

"Aye?" She looked at the neatly stacked proof pages in the expectation that he would suggest a new approach.

"Not about the book—about you."

"Me?" She had been everything candid, she hoped.

And so was he. "Prepare yourself, Miss Elspeth Otis, to be wooed."

This time, the smile on her face matched the warm feeling within.

She should like nothing better.

Chapter 12

HAMISH APPLIED HIMSELF to the wooing of Miss Elspeth Otis with the same single-minded enthusiasm he had heretofore reserved only for his business ventures.

He said no more of lessons or kisses, but set about inspiring the imaginative flights of fancy that would inspire so fey and remarkable a creature as his Elspeth. And *his* Elspeth he vowed she was, from the top of her flaxen head to the tip of her well-worn shoes.

And more well-worn they became under his direction, for every day he endeavored to show her a different sight, or experience, or view of his beloved, bustling, ancient city, from the highest battlement of the Castle to the belfry of Canongate Kirk.

He didn't mind when she would pause, wide-eyed, to scribble some passage in a well-worn notebook, or stop to sketch a fox that crossed their path half-way up to Arthur's Seat, or a hare in the bramble at the foot of Calton Hill. He didn't interrupt when the vista across Dudingston Loch inspired her raptures, and the dark, echoing closes moved her to silence.

And he never, not once, even attempted to kiss her.

But he thought about it—about the pliant texture of her sweet lips—every moment of every day, though Lady Ivers most often accompanied them on their daily journeys.

He thought of kissing Elspeth when he took her hand to help her up some steep hill, or down a curving stair. He thought about kissing Elspeth while he basked in the glow of her smile, and rested in the cool shade of her intellect. He thought of kissing Elspeth in his sleep.

He thought about her until he began to think he was no longer capable of thinking about anything else. Until he thought he might go mad from the wanting of her.

Until, at long last, they chanced to find themselves alone.

Hamish had returned with her, flush-faced and relaxed from their exercise, to her aunt's home, and while Elspeth collapsed happily into an arm chair, still in the thrall of some revel, Lady Ivers took a letter from the tray in the hall, and excused herself.

"Call for refreshments, if you would, Elspeth. I won't be but a moment to answer this missive…"

"Hmm," Elspeth agreed, but made no move for the bell.

The door latch clicked into place behind Lady Ivers, and there he was, alone with a beautiful young woman with her eyes closed and her head tipped back to catch a sunbeam, as if she were just waiting for his lips to finally find hers. "Elspeth."

She turned her head at the sound of his voice, and it was as if the very air in the room became charged with the force of their attraction.

"Yes, Hamish?" Her voice was quiet in a way that felt something more than private. Something more decidedly secret. Something intimate.

"I wondered, " he asked as he walked slowly toward her. "If perhaps, I might try again?"

"Try what again?" she asked. But she knew—her whisper was nothing but breath and hope.

"Try kissing," he answered on an echoing whisper. "I've been waiting very patiently to find the right moment for another lesson in kissing."

Her smile was all in her luminous eyes. "So have I."

He wanted to fall upon her, to subsume himself in her

scent and softness, but he knew better. He also knew how to make the exquisite anticipation last.

"Perhaps I ought to ask you, properly, first?"

"Ask what?"

"Ask if I might be so bold as to give you a kiss?"

Her only answer was a smile as warm and inviting as that sunbeam.

Hamish eased himself to one knee beside her chair, and she reached out to him.

His hands stole to her cheek, and the sensation that slid deep into his gut might well be described as his own sort of awakening—Hamish felt his heart was beating so loudly in anticipation, she must be able to hear it.

But there she was—this warm, willing, winsome young woman—smiling shyly at him, as if she shared none of his agitation.

As if he were offering her her own heart's desire.

He brushed his lips against hers—once, twice. Softly, so softly he could feel the gentle exhalation of her sigh against his cheek. His other hand stole around her nape, pulling her closer as his thumb fanned along the line of her jaw, angling and tipping her head back so they could kiss more deeply. So he could taste the summer wind on her tongue, and smell the sprig of hedge roses she had tucked into her hair.

"Hamish." She breathed his name against his skin, and it was as if he were instantly set alight—as if every inch of his body came to aroused, prickling awareness of just how much he wanted this woman. Just how much he was prepared to give, and give up, for her.

Her hands slid around his neck, holding him to her, binding him more surely than a tether. Deepening their contact, and their connection. He could smell the rose scent on her flesh. He could feel the warmth of her skin against his lips. He could hear the ever so slightly strained rasp of his breath mingle with hers.

But it felt vastly different from when he had kissed her— his senses felt heightened, as if she were the one teaching him. As if he were the naïve provincial being tutored in the wicked ways of the world.

And just as she was about to withdraw, he turned his head, just so.

Just so their mouths fit against each other, and their lips meshed as if by design. As if they had always been meant to do so.

AFTER THE UNBRIDLED exuberance of their first kiss, the second kiss was a marked contrast—a careful exploration that slowly gave way to something else. Something gentler. Something far more personal. Elspeth let her eyes flutter closed, overwhelmed by the newness and wonder of it all. Something that had to be joy broke loose from her heart.

Because now she knew why the Aunts had warned and warned her.

Because that simple touch, that merest brush of a lover's lips against her own felt so good, so right, and so necessary, a reckless, breathlessness pleasure rose within her, swamping every last bit of her good sense.

But his sense appeared to be fully functioning—he pulled away, silently scooting his chair over. "Footsteps, sweet Elspeth."

Hamish—for it would be foolish to stand on formality and call a man she had just kissed Mr. Cathcart—stood but kept careful hold of her hand, moving his thumb lightly back and forth across her palm. The simple contact sent a shiver skittering under the surface of her skin, shocking her in a way that his kisses hadn't.

"You're so lovely." He leaned in as he spoke, making vague murmuring sounds of ease as he gently brushed his lips against the curve of her jaw under her ear. "Clever, sweet Elspeth."

Oh, she felt that simple touch all the way to her fingertips and the tips of her toes. And beyond—her skin fairly radiated with the wave of sensation emanating from the spot where his lips pressed, taut and firm, full of easy, gentle promise.

He moved away from her just as Aunt Augusta sailed through the door.

"And that, my dear children," her aunt decreed, "is more than enough work for one afternoon."

"I hadn't realized it had gotten so late." Elspeth rose from her chair, and tried to school both her fluster and her disappointment behind obedience, just as she always had.

But Hamish Cathcart wasn't even trying to hide his smile—he had such warm pleasure in his eyes, that she stopped trying so very hard to hide her elation.

Kissing, she decided, had been vastly underrated, and grossly underappreciated at Dove Cottage. Luckily for her, she was not there anymore. She was in Edinburgh, in a new life with a new aunt.

Who shooed Hamish out. "I regret it is time for you to take your leave, Hamish. I have let you have your way with Elspeth's time, but this evening I mean to make up for all the evenings she has spent in the service of your manuscripts. I have pledged us—Elspeth and I—for an intimate ball at the home of the Countess of Inverness. A most satisfactory, charming ball that will not be one of those sad, mad crushes that are all the rage in London—and I must have my beautiful niece with me. And she must be suitably dressed."

"Oh." Elspeth's sunny mood dimmed. She hated to bring the thorn of practicality in the side of such a rosy prospect, but they had accomplished nothing of what they had set out to do. "But—"

"No buts, my darling Elspeth." Aunt Augusta raised one perfectly shaped brow to silence all protest. "Say good day to Mr. Cathcart."

Hamish took his cue, bowing to her curtsey in the most gentlemanly manner. "Lady Ivers. My dear Miss Otis." She fancied that his smile was broader still when he kissed her hand. "Until we meet again." And with one barely perceptible wink he was gone, out the front door and down the steps without looking back.

Elspeth knew this because she ran to the window of the

drawing room to watch.

"We'll see him again shortly, my love," Aunt Augusta advised. "And it won't do to let him see you pine." But then her expression narrowed. "Or perhaps it is time to give your Mr. Cathcart some reason to pine." Her cat-in-cream smile was her decision. "Yes. I'll have my dresser pick out something utterly divine for you to wear to your first ball. She'll have it pressed and aired and be waiting to dress your hair—very simply, for it is divine and needs only a pinch of powder—while we have a bite to eat. Pray pull for the footman, Elspeth, and then come and sit with me in my dressing room to sup and be transformed."

"But—" Elspeth fought against the instinct—or rather the twenty-odd years of being taught strictly not to call attention to herself—to protest. Because she had always stayed at home when others had gone to the few local assemblies the neighborhood had afforded. She had always sat quietly on visits, never putting herself forward. She had always hidden her disappointments behind duty.

But this was a new life, in which she could put herself forward. In which she could wear silk and be transformed. She could go to a ball.

Even if she couldn't dance a step.

Aunt Augusta took the excuses from her. "Don't think you can stand against me, my darling lass, for I always get my way." She laid a warm hand upon Elspeth's cold fingers. "You need not worry, my dear, that I mean to make you over into someone else—you are perfectly lovely just as you are. But you will be something more than lovely once we can pry off all the fusty layers of middle-aged morality Molly and Isla have buried you under. Somewhere beneath the weight of all those scruples and self-doubt is your mother's beauty, just waiting to shine."

"But I don't know how to act—I've never been to a ball like—"

"There is nothing to it, my darling," Aunt Augusta assured her. "You have only to be yourself."

Elspeth's relief was as profound as her worry—she had

never been allowed, much less encouraged, to be herself. But a ball seemed an excellent place to begin.

Chapter 13

THE BALL WAS to take place at the Countess of Inverness's stately mansion on the Canongate High Street. If Elspeth had found the gracious elegance of her aunt's townhouse a wonder, the gilded, candlelit opulence of Inverness House was a sight beyond compare. She had never imagined such a profusion of candelabra, glinting gold against the stuccoed and painted walls, nor such a press of richly dressed people.

Elspeth bobbed along in her aunt's wake, feeling like a gawky gosling paddling after a swan—Aunt Augusta was a vision in palest French lilac and white powder, and even though Elspeth knew she herself had never looked so lovely in all her life, she had nothing of her aunt's ease and grace.

Still, she could learn. She could follow her aunt's elegant example, and nod and smile and bow her head graciously. She could look over the crowd for a certain tall gentleman without craning her neck as if she were the veriest bumpkin. She could pretend that this was how she had always lived, in luxury and light, and always would.

"There you are, dear Letty." Aunt Augusta kissed their hostess on the cheek. "Let me introduce my dear niece and protégée, Miss Elspeth Otis. Elspeth, I give you the Countess of Inverness, my dear friend Letty."

"What a delightful girl, Gussie. Welcome, my dear." The countess turned to Elspeth with every appearance of gracious delight. "A pleasure to have you with us, Miss Otis."

Elspeth sank into a deeply reverential curtsey. "My lady."

"Such graceful manners, Augusta. We must have her dancing. The gentlemen will be all agog to have a chance with her."

"We shall be excessively selective, Letty. Only the best will do for my darling girl."

"I see." The two women turned to survey the floor, much like Elspeth imagined generals might do when surveying the field of battle. "The Marquess of Cairn is here, just up from London." The countess gestured with her fan to an imposing gentleman in crimson velvet.

"Ah, yes." Those mischievous dimples appeared deep in Aunt Augusta's subtly rouged cheeks. "Perfection. Let us take ourselves in the marquess's direction."

AND THAT, CLEARLY, was Hamish's cue. Elspeth Otis was his discovery, his diamond in the rough, and under no circumstance could he stand to lose her to his charming brother Rory's even more charming crony, Alasdair Strathcairn, Marquess of Cairn. Because in the hours between leaving Lady Ivers's house and arriving at the ball this evening, Hamish had been unable to think of anything or anyone but Elspeth.

And her kisses.

"My ladies." Hamish swept in, taking the hands the ladies instinctively and automatically proffered when he bowed before them. "Countess Inverness, Lady Ivers. And Miss Otis." He bowed particularly reverentially before the object of his increasingly devoted attention, who looked like a breath of sweet summer sky in a blue silk gown the deep color of the ocean. "What a pleasant surprise."

Lady Ivers didn't look in the least bit surprised. "Mr. Cathcart. Your timing is impeccable, as always."

Hamish took the backhanded compliment in the spirit it was intended—as a challenge. Time was of the essence. "My dear Miss Otis, might I beg the honor of this dance?"

The darling lass looked halfway between horrified and delighted. "Of course you may beg, much good it will do either of us. You see, I'm afraid I cannot—"

"Of course you can." Lady Ivers looked from Elspeth to Hamish in shrewd assessment, before she decided to voice her full consent. "Mr. Cathcart is harmless enough, Elspeth. I see no reason why you should not dance with him, provided he behaves himself. And I shall watch quite closely to make sure that he does."

Hamish bowed deeply to acknowledge the warning. "As you wish, my lady." He offered Elspeth his hand. Which she did not take. In fact, she looked at his proffered palm the way a wee mousie might eye a rat.

"Come now," he laughed. "'Tis only a country dance, my dear Miss Otis, not the end of the world."

"Not yet, anyway." But she let him lead her toward the dance floor. Toward, but not exactly *to*—she held back at the edge of the crowd.

"Forgive me if I notice some hesitation on your part, Miss Otis. If the trouble is not with me—and what trouble could there be with a fellow of my charming sort—then it must be you. Is there some difficulty?"

"Yes. There is a great difficulty. Not *exactly* with me, but with the dance."

"*The Montgomery's Rant?* 'Tis a simple dance." But at her continued frown he was prompted to ask, "You do know how to dance, do you not, Elspeth? Even if there was no kissing, surely there were dances even in whatever wee benighted village you came from?"

His tease had at least a little of the desired effect—she crushed her lips between her teeth in an effort not to smile. "I am quite sound on the *theory*. And assemblies were held in the public rooms of the village inn—which while not exactly benighted, I will acknowledge were a trifle dim—the very grand sum of four times a year—"

"Four times? So many as that?" His own pleasure was all in her arch sweetness. "I begin to see your trouble. Not exactly a whirlwind social calendar."

"No," she agreed. "I am also forced to admit"—she lowered her voice, as if imparting the greatest of confidences—"they often have to invite the whole of the hedgerows, including the badgers, in order to have enough couples for a proper set. So I ought to be well used to dancing with *your* sort." She took a deep breath, and peeped up at him from the corner of her eye. "But the real truth of the matter is that while I have danced imaginary dances with real badgers, and real dances with imaginary people, I have never danced a real dance with a real, live, handsome gentleman of your sort, or any other."

He could not help but smile at such sweetly charming flattery. "I think you'll find gentlemen differ from blacksmiths and farmers only in the cut of their clothes and not in their appreciation of the dance. Or of their partners."

A lovely flush swept across her cheeks. "You are very kind to misunderstand me, Hamish. But let me be more plainspoken." She stood on tiptoe to impart the whispered confidence. "I have *never* danced."

"What do you mean?" Hamish was beyond astonished— it was one thing not to have been kissed, but never to dance as well? "Not once?"

"Shh," she implored, before she admitted, "Not ever."

Something strange and fine and indignant stirred to life within his chest—a sort of inchoate rage that anyone might ever have slighted this creature by not asking her to dance. "Why the hell not?"

Please." She glanced around to see if they were being overheard. "Circumstances simply didn't permit—"

No kissing, no dancing—who knew what else she'd been denied. Which made her writing all the more remarkable. *She* was remarkable.

"What a marvelously mixed up world you've lived in, dear Elspeth. My duty is clear—you don't need lessons in kissing, but you do need lessons in dancing. But we shall need somewhere more private than this crowded floor for your first lesson." He put out his hand. "Come with me."

Chapter 14

HAMISH HAD A moment of worry while she looked at his hand as if she might refuse such a blunt offer. "There is a garden at the back with some greater room to maneuv—" But perhaps that was not the best way of putting it either. "I'm sure you'll find it refreshing."

The frown across her forehead eased. "Yes. Thank you. Aunt Augusta said the ball would not be a mad crush, but …"

Indeed, there were people everywhere in the cavernous old mansion—ladies coming and going from the withdrawing room, gentlemen filling the card room with smoke, couples tucking themselves away into every nook and niche intent upon more than private conversation.

He steered her through the crowd, aiming for a more private way out of the house to the garden he knew lay beyond, worried that the press of bodies might be a bit much for Elspeth, whose eyes were growing as big as tea saucers from staring at all the carryings-on with a sort of curious wonder he was coming to recognize as particular to her character—she looked as if she'd like to take out her little pocket notebook and make sketches.

"Did you see that?" she gasped, pulling him aside. "I think I just saw a young lady cut the buttons from that man's coat," she reported.

Hamish followed her gaze to see Alasdair Strathcairn, Marquess of Cairn engaged in a rather tense-looking conversation with the youngest of the Winthrop girls. "Are you sure?"

"I think so—at least his coat doesn't have any buttons in the back, though I could swear it did when the countess wanted to introduce us."

The last thing Hamish wanted was his Elspeth contemplating her missed introduction to the marquess. "Ah, well—serve him right. About time someone took Alasdair Strathcairn down a peg."

"You don't think it's wrong?"

"I think it's more likely a joke on auld Alasdair. I think that's Edinburgh for ye." He winked to show her he was joking as well, but Hamish still whisked her out the door, beyond the reach of the dashing marquesses of the world— he wanted her to himself.

Elspeth stepped into lamp-lit back garden with palpable relief. "Oh, thank you. This is so much better." The garden was sheltered from the worst of the changeable Scottish weather by a high brick wall crowded with vines and Scotch roses just budding into flower. "It smells heavenly."

"And much less like the rest of this reeking auld city?" Hamish led her farther along the fine stone path, holding to his side of the walkway, and keeping his hands well to himself. Not thinking about the pale swath of flesh above the wide scooped neckline of her gown.

In short—very gentlemanly. Because she was, indeed, a wee, fey, innocent country mousie, and not the arch, knowing creature he had wished her to be.

But she was neither—she was her own wonderful, surprising self, because she slid her hand into his as if it were the most natural thing in the world. As if she wanted the simple contact of palm to palm as much as he. "Oh, Hamish, this is wonderful. I have always wanted to dance."

And he, it seemed had always wanted to dance with her. "I am honored." He aligned himself across from her and bowed deeply.

"And I curtsey." She made him a swanlike reverence.

"You most certainly do—very well. And now we step forward and take hands—"

She mirrored his movement easily, and very gracefully followed him into the next.

Already they were dancing. "You are either a very quick study, Elspeth Otis, or you have been bamming me just to get me alone with you in the dark."

"No!" Her cheeks pinked. "I used to watch—through the windows—and listen to the music. And perhaps try out a step or two in the garden, when no one was looking. The badgers like a partner now and again."

It was an image of such aching poignancy that he could not keep himself from drawing her closer than the dance prescribed. "Elspeth." He drew her hand to his lips. "I will be your badger this evening."

Dimples appeared at the corners of her sweet mouth. "I'm not sure you have the requisite whiskers."

He held her hand to his chest and hoped she could not feel the pounding of his pulse. "Should you like to find out?"

Her upturned mouth was right there, soft and open just the barest amount—ready for his kiss. But he would not take. With Elspeth he would offer.

"Will you—" Her cheeks flushed a rosier shade of pink. "Do you think you might like to…kiss me?"

"Ye gods, yes." Hamish had to close his eyes against the anticipatory rush of pleasure her words set loose inside him—experienced she might not be, but spirited, she certainly was. "My dear Elspeth, I should like nothing more."

And to prove it to her, and because he was an unsteady, rash, ramshackle third son who most often did as he liked, he kissed her.

He kissed her with all the impatience that had brewed in his gut since the moment he had entered the ball and laid eyes upon the sweet swath of skin revealed by the low cut of her gown—what in hell was Augusta Ivers thinking to encourage the oglers so? He kissed her with all the pent-up joy and passion and hope and attraction roiling within him. He kissed her because he was a lad and she was a lass, and she was sweet and willing and eager for exactly what he wanted—more.

More of the sweet taste of her. More of the smooth touch of her skin. More of the heavenly bliss that obliterated every other thought. She tasted sweet, she felt alive, and she did not push him away.

Instead she had latched on to the lapels of his coat as if she could not yet get close enough.

But he would oblige her—he slid his arm around the small of her back and tugged her so close he could feel the stern press of her stays against his belly. The pressure sent a jolt of want shuddering through him.

He had to work to curb the impulse to turn her around and press her into the wall, and rake his hands through her carefully arranged *coiffure*.

Because then there'd be hell to pay. And everything put paid to their plans.

But what was so wrong about that? They could make new plans.

Still, he gentled his approach, murmuring easy words of pleasure. "Elspeth. So soft. So sweet." Enticing without overwhelming. Inviting her to kiss him back without doing anything more.

But it was hard, so hard to maintain control when her lids fluttered shut, and she melted against his chest. "Oh, aye."

She tasted like apples and clean fresh water. She tasted like ease and simplicity and everything perfect and right. She tasted like a summer evening's soft breeze and a night full of dancing stars. And she was holding on to him—her hands fisted in the lapels of his coat—just as tenaciously as he was holding on to her, that he didn't care about innocence or experience. He only cared about deepening the kiss. About tracing the lush curve of her back, and wrapping his arm around her waist to pull her flush into his chest. About cupping the back of her head to angle her jaw just enough to deepen the kiss and sweep his tongue into her mouth to slake his thirst for the tart taste of her.

"I knew it," he breathed as he moved to kiss the sensitive

tendon at the sweet slide of her neck. "I knew the lass who had written those words and thought those thoughts would kiss like a dream. I knew under that guarded, innocent exterior would beat the wild, daring heart of a poet. I knew."

He brought his mouth back to her soft lips, already missing her, already hungry for another taste of her lips, another drink of her shyly questing tongue. Wanting to discover just what it was that made him hold her like he never meant to let her go.

And not even that particularly dangerous thought could keep him from sliding his fingers into her artfully arranged hair, disrupting pins that pattered like raindrops onto the path as he let the smooth strands slide through his hands. "Elspeth." Her name was like a gift he gave himself, an incantation that transported him to places unknown. Places of lush wonder and graceful, careless ease—a garden of "Elspeth."

"Hamish. My own." Her answering whisper was filled with that characteristic wonder, and a little bewilderment, as if she had not yet decided if this were really happening. If they really were kissing like experienced lovers trysting in the dark of the garden.

They most assuredly were.

And he wanted to do more.

He drew her hard against his chest, wishing she were wearing less, cursing that he was wearing even more. He wanted to peel off his cravat and waistcoat, and tear off his linen shirt so he could feel the febrile heat of her body flush against his skin, and taste more than just the flesh of her lips.

He skated his mouth down the long slide of her swanlike neck to the warm hollow of her collarbone, and she tipped her head away, tacitly granting him access. His hands followed where his lips led, rounding over her shoulders, pushing aside the whispering silk of her sleeves, brushing aside the fall of lace that edged her bodice.

The lovely curve of her breasts filled his palm, and he wanted more, wanted to feel the weight of her in his hands. Wanted to see and taste the pink tips hidden beneath soft chemise and tight-laced stays.

He put his mouth to her sweet, satin-smooth skin just above the upper edge of her chemise, and she gasped with the same wonder and delight and joy that he felt to be with her, and alone. His own body responded to hers in the most primitive, savagely pleasurable way, and it was everything he could do to keep himself from backing her against the ivy-covered wall. To keep himself from taking down the rest of her bodice, and hiking up her skirts to give them both a greater taste of paradise.

But he could not.

Because she was not only sweet Elspeth Otis, the adored niece of Lady Augusta Ivers, and deserved better, but he was Mr. Hamish Cathcart, of a long and mostly-noble lineage and a moral code of his own. One he meant to keep.

Chapter 15

"DARLING ELSPETH," HAMISH'S lips pressed against her forehead, and then dotted down the line of her nose to her mouth. Which she opened to give him—

"Well, well. What have we here? Found a bit of muslin you'd like to share, Cathcart?"

The words, uttered by a different deep male voice, only half-penetrated the fog of pleasure permeating Elspeth's brain.

But Hamish immediately thrust her from his arms, pushing her behind him as he simultaneously stepped in front of her, blocking the man's view. "Bànach." There was a definite chill in Hamish's voice. "Make yourself scarce."

"And miss all the fun? Nay." Elspeth could hear the man's snide smile.

But Hamish could see it as well. "Bànach."

The cold threat in Hamish's voice was enough to move the man off, but not before Elspeth heard him mutter. "Like father, like daughter, eh? Sorry I didn't get to that one first."

Elspeth had never been so mortified in all her life—and the Aunts Murray had regularly mortified her in the name of keeping her from being "too proud."

"I'm sorry for that," Hamish said as he stooped to gather hairpins. "I suppose it's just as well."

"Just as well?" How could any part of public humiliation be *just as well*?

Elspeth moved as far away as the low privet hedge bordering the path would allow, taking some small comfort that Hamish seemed just as exercised as she—she could hear his breath sawing in and out of his chest.

Her own breath was just as unruly—she was as winded as if she had run all the way round the orchard. Twice. Before the interruption she would have thought his kisses well worth the trip—her lips still throbbed and her cheeks still tingled with the sensation of his rougher skin against hers.

"Devil take it. Someone else is—" Hamish stepped abruptly away, scattering hairpins on the ground in his haste.

"My dear?" Aunt Augusta's careful voice floated up the path. "Is that you?"

Elspeth's hands flew to her hair, trying to twist and jab pins back into some semblance of order, but it was too late.

"I was just given an alarming report." Aunt Augusta took in the two of them at a glance. "No need to ask you two darling children if it were true."

"We were just—"

"Talking," Hamish finished.

"Of the book," Elspeth clarified.

"Books," Hamish corrected. "Miss Otis and I were discussing some of the difficulties she has been having with the revision."

"Indeed?" Aunt Augusta's tone was as dry as it was amused. "From what I saw, there didn't look to be any difficulties at all."

"Michty me." Elspeth couldn't possibly maintain her composure. Not with her aunt's clear-eyed gaze taking in each detail of her mussed hair and clothing. Elspeth tugged her gown back into place upon her shoulder. "Please forgive me. I don't know what came over me."

"Mr. Cathcart, one can only suppose, came over you," was Aunt Augusta's wry response. "And your own natural human nature. You've proved yourself to be a faster learner than I would have given you credit for, dear child." Her aunt mercifully turned her keen gaze upon Hamish. "And you, Hamish Cathcart. Letting no grass grow, I see. Well, my dears, what a pretty pickle you seem to have gotten yourselves into."

"Your ladyship." For the first time in their—albeit short—acquaintance, Hamish Cathcart's face was flushed with riddy color. "My apologies."

"I am not the one to whom you should apologize. You young men today—always in such a rush." Aunt Augusta shook her head as she took the hairpins from his hand. "My niece has been acquainted with you but a few weeks, Cathcart. To attempt seduction at her first ball, before she's even had a chance to dance." She gave the two of them such an exasperated sigh, Elspeth began to feel ashamed of her own concealment.

If the Aunts could see her, they would be horrified. Even without their censure, she was heartily ashamed of herself. "It wasn't entirely Mr. Cathcart's fault, Aunt Augusta." Her first true beau, and she had abandoned all the principles she had been brought up with. One moonlit ball, and she had thrown herself at the first man to offer her any attention.

"Nay." Hamish quickly contradicted her. "Your aunt is right. But Elspeth, you must know I meant no disrespect. Quite the opposite. My feelings quite carried me away."

"Yes. They seem to do that to you, don't they?" Aunt Augusta would not make it easy for him. "Well, let them carry you off for the remainder of the evening, so we'll have no more public displays of over-affection. I must speak to my niece."

Hamish bowed to the inevitable. "As you wish, my lady." He bowed to her aunt, and then turned to take Elspeth's suddenly chilly hand—she was suddenly anxious not to be parted from him.

But he seemed just as anxious for their next meeting as she. "Elspeth, if I may, I'll call on you tomorrow, so we might discuss our further plans."

"I—" She did not know what to say, or where to look.

But he either didn't hear her distress, or ignored it. "Then it is set." He bowed once more. "Good evening." He strode off through the crowd, leaving Elspeth to repair the damage to her coiffure.

"I am afraid, dear Elspeth, that you may not be able to make the appointment with Mr. Cathcart."

Elspeth heard the censure in her aunt's voice. "I am so very sorry, Aunt Augusta. Truly. But I thought you liked Mr. Cathcart—I thought you were perhaps even encouraging—"

"Indeed I do like him. And indeed I was encouraging. But it is all for naught." Aunt Augusta drew near enough to take Elspeth's hand, and she saw then what she had not before— the strain making fine tense lines across her aunt's face.

"Whatever is it?"

"Reeves, my butler, has just come with a message. It arrived express, not an hour ago. Your Aunt Molly Murray has written. Your Aunt Isla is ill, gravely so, and has asked for you."

A pain that felt like the rending of her heart stopped Elspeth's breath. Here she had been learning to flirt and kiss and dance, and all the while her dear aunt lay dying.

Elspeth had never felt more selfish or more bereft in her life. All thought but one fled. "I must go to her. I must go home to Dove Cottage."

HAMISH PRESENTED HIMSELF in St. Andrew Square the next afternoon at precisely two o'clock—the earliest time he reckoned Lady Ivers would conscience a morning call—to make his most handsome apologies. He was immediately shown into the lady's private parlor.

"Come in, Hamish, come in. There is much to be done. We've made a hash of it, you and I." This Lady Ivers said with some accusation.

A cold drop of consciousness dripped down the back of his neck—his kissing had never been labeled a *hash*. "How so, my lady?"

"She's gone." Lady Ivers threw up her hands. "Packed up

and whisked herself away, called back to their bolt-hole in the hedgerows by the illness of one of the sisters Murray, her decrepit, selfish aunts in the hinterlands of Midlothian. Though it might as well be Mongolia, for all that."

Hamish controlled his smile at her wry tone. "Most of Midlothian is but a morning's carriage ride away, my lady. Entirely approachable."

"Good! Then I trust you shall be taking that carriage ride *and* making that approach as soon as possible? We must get her back or all my schemes for her happiness are come to naught. Poor child—she's as sharp and clever as a cleaver, but rather naïve. She still has no idea that I sent her the manuscript of a purpose, to bring her here. And even, once I saw the rapport between the two of you, to send her your way."

Hamish had surmised as much but hadn't wanted to jump to any assumptions. "I am honored."

"And so you should be. You're a clever lad, Hamish—you have a way of seeing beyond what needs to be done. You can imagine what *might be.*"

"I am deeply honored, my lady."

"Yes, yes. But find her," Lady Ivers ordered. "Go to her, and press your offer, without"—she raised her voice in emphasis—"getting things as all mangled up in *amour* as you managed to do last night. There is time enough for all the kissing in the world *after* you have secured her." She faced him squarely. "Get her back here for me, Cathcart. Find her and win her, please. My happiness depends upon it."

"As does mine, my lady. As does mine."

Chapter 16

"ELSPETH? ELSPETH, ARE you listening to me?"

The insistent query penetrated the sad fog of her brain only an instant before Aunt Isla gave her a swift poke in the side. "Yes, Aunt, I'm listening."

Isla's lined pink face was puckered with worry and disapproval, though she seemed otherwise to have recovered rather miraculously from her brush with mortality—this morning she was well enough to take a glass of milk, and come out of her room so she might supervise Elspeth's work from a chair under the arbor. "Your attention has been everywhere but on your tasks. Had your head turned in the city, I've no doubt," she sighed. "Telling you all sorts of falsehoods—like your parents being married. Unforgivable."

Elspeth sighed to cover the humiliation that threatened to overwhelm her like the runaway rose pulling over the arbor. "Yes, Aunt."

It hadn't been her head that had been turned, but another, less intelligent part of her body. Which might have been her heart.

Or something even more susceptible.

But she couldn't tell Aunt Isla *that*, now could she? "I did not have my head turned by the city, Aunt Isla," she tried to reassure her. "Indeed, I came home because I much prefer the quiet life, here, where everything is comfortable and cozy and easy."

Or so she had kept telling herself for the past four days. Over and over as she did her chores, tidying the parlor, shaking out the rugs, or pouring the weak, watery tea. Over and over as she dutifully sang hymns at Morningsong, or walked stolidly home from the kirk, or drew water from the well.

And especially in the lush garden, full of color and scent, when she leaned back against the sun-warmed wall, and her body remembered the feel of his braw strength pressed tight and strong to hers. The warmth of his chest. The span of his hands as he had cupped her head and kissed her lips—

"Elspeth!"

Elspeth looked at the rose blossom she had just lopped off, fallen at her feet. "I'm sorry, Aunt." And she was sorry. Sorry that Isla's worry that Elspeth would leave for Edinburgh again made her so snappish and fretful. Sorry that she wanted to leave anyway, even when she knew how badly it discommoded the Aunts, who really did need her home.

"What on earth ails you, child?"

"Nothing, Aunt." Nothing that the courage of her convictions and a far greater share of daring would not cure.

"And what is that infernal noise? That shrill—"

Elspeth stopped long enough to listen—on the other side of the garden wall, someone in the lane was whistling. Loudly.

Aunt Isla stretched up like a hare to peer around the hedge. "It's some ramshackle fellow, lounging along the fence like a reprobate. Like to steal us blind if we let him."

A jolt of terrible pleasure bolted into her veins, and shot Elspeth onto her tiptoes to keek over the wall. Because the ramshackle fellow at the gate was none other than Mr. Hamish Cathcart. Who looked likely to steal only kisses.

He had come. He had come for her.

Her joy and excitement made her skittish with hope. "I'll just go see what he wants, shall I?" Elspeth didn't wait for the permission she knew would not come, but bolted over the wall.

"Elspeth!" Aunt Isla clung to her like a cobweb. "Your ankles. And you forgot your cap!"

The dratted lace mobcap hung like a hangman's cowl from her aunt's fingers. "Thank you, Aunt." Elspeth reached back for it because she knew she must, but rather than put it on her head, she folded it deep into her pocket. "I don't want to dirty it with my soil."

Elspeth closed the gate firmly behind her, wiped her suddenly damp palms on her apron, and tried to speak as if her heart weren't hammering against her ears like the blacksmith's anvil—*he had come, he had come*. "Mr. Cathcart."

"My very dear Miss Otis." He smiled, tipped his hat, and glanced around as if he were not quite sure of his welcome. "Fancy meeting you here."

"Fancy that, indeed." It made her irrationally happy to see him again. "How did you find me?"

"Lady Ivers set my course." He gave her that roguishly self-deprecating grin. "And once I found the village, I inquired of the badgers, who were surprisingly tight-lipped about your whereabouts. But your neighbors"—he nodded back down the lane where two women pretended not to be straining to hear their conversation from their own listing gates—"were kindly more forthcoming."

They had a veritable crowd for Twelve Mile Burn village—her own relations strained and peered over the wall at her back.

"What does he want, Elspeth?" Aunt Molly had joined Isla in the garden, their noses practically twitching like march hares. "Tell him to go away!"

"Yes, Auntie." Elspeth hardly knew where to look—at his lovely hands that had held her tight, or his lovely warm brown eyes that crinkled at the corners with humor, or that smiling mouth that had once covered hers with bliss. "I'm afraid you're to go away."

"I heard." He tipped his hat cordially toward the garden wall. "But I don't think I shall. Not when I've come all this way to find you." His voice got a little quieter. "You ran away."

Elspeth felt her face flame so hot it was a wonder she didn't go up in a puff of white smoke right in the middle of the lane, like some fairy tale witch. If only he would not look at her so—with that charming gleam at the corner of his eye, as if he were thinking about the last time they had been together. As if he were just waiting her word to lead her into another secluded garden.

But the nearest secluded garden contained the Aunts, who were unfortunately right about her—she had a weakness, it seemed, for rogues.

"I didn't really mean to run away." It only seemed fair to give him the truth. "But my Aunt Isla was deathly ill."

He looked over at the Aunts, bristling with hostility and rude health. "She seems quite recovered."

"Aye, but—"

"So why haven't you come back?"

Elspeth didn't have a ready answer, though she had asked herself the same question over and over once it was clear her Aunt Isla was, indeed, going to recover. But she also remembered the degradation of being called "a bit of muslin," as if she were no more than a rag. The familiar mortified heat suffused her face. "I didn't belong there, Mr. Cathcart. I was…out of my depth."

"Out of your depth? Elspeth Otis." His voice was as teasing as it was chiding. "I think you hadn't even begun to plumb your own depths."

"Elspeth? Elspeth!"

This time, the cry from the garden held real alarm. And only Aunt Molly's head was visible on the other side of the wall.

Elspeth immediately vaulted the wall with no care for her ankles. Aunt Isla lay in a heap on the grass path—Aunt Molly was at her side cradling her head.

"Did she fall?"

"Fainted." Aunt Molly's voice was thin with concern. "Her heart is just not strong."

Elspeth took Isla's wrist and felt her reedy pulse in confirmation. There was no need to tell her that it was she who had upset her aunt's fragile health by entertaining roguish gentlemen in the lane.

But that roguish gentleman had evidently followed her over the garden wall, and was even now bending down to take the frail old woman into his arms. "Show me where to take her."

Elspeth could only point the way through the single French door into the tiny back parlor and hope that the terrible thrill of being carried by such a man wouldn't send poor Isla to her grave. "On the settee. I'll get her hartshorn."

"It's in her pockets," Aunt Molly instructed from the doorway, as if she were too afraid of Hamish's rather overwhelming presence—his head nearly scraped the timbers of the low parlor ceiling—to even attend to her sister.

"I found it." Elspeth knelt by the side of the settee to waive the vial in front of her aunt's pale nose. "Take a deep breath, Aunt Isla."

"Oh my." Isla's thin black lashes fluttered open. And then she set eyes on Hamish hovering behind Elspeth. "Oooh, no!"

She had to get him out. "Thank you for your assistance, Mr. Cath— Sir," she amended, as she gestured back the way they had come. "If you'd just wait outside?"

It took a delicate bit of maneuvering to usher Aunt Molly out of the doorway and over to the settee so Hamish could go out, but it was soon enough accomplished. "I'm afraid you'll have to leave."

Hamish grinned even as he shook his head. "After coming all this way to find you? Not a chance."

"But you must. Your mere presence—"

"Yes, I see. But if you cannot leave—and I see that you can't—then I must remain. Until I can convince you."

"Convince me of what?"

"That you belong in Edinburgh. With me."

A different sort of heat swept down her throat, and headed for those lower depths. "Wheesht!" She cast a worried glance over her shoulder at both the Aunts, who might be dying, or at the very least aging rapidly, but still had ears like hungry barn cats.

"What is he still doing here, Elspeth? What does he want?"

"He's looking for work, Aunt. Gardening and the like." It was the only thing she could think of at a moment's notice that might be plausible—as long as the Aunts hadn't taken too close a look at Mr. Cathcart's ink-smudged hands.

"Aye, mistress," Hamish raised his voice and answered for himself, cheerfully tipping his hat again to the ladies of the house. "Looking for a bit of honest work."

"Don't have any work for vagrants." Aunt Molly's tone was firm.

"You'd know best, mistress," he answered, all charming Scots fealty. "Tho' a mon can't help notice ye've a powerful lot o' repairs that need doin' to the place—that eave looks dicey, and ye stand in certain need o' new thatch. I could have the whole of it patched and as snug as a sealskin within an afternoon. And take a good pruning to that runaway rosebush, as well."

The Aunts turned as one to look through the window at the rose that looked as if it were making a meal of the rickety arbor. Somehow, he had managed to hit upon a topic guaranteed to play to her Aunts' pride—they had always taken great care in the upkeep of their cottage and garden, but as the years had gone on and their vigor had been sapped and their finances had slowly dwindled, things couldn't be as meticulously maintained as before.

But the idea that he—this earl's son from Edinburgh— would actually do such work was comical. "Laying it on a bit thick, aren't you?" she warned in a whisper. "You can't possibly know anything about thatch."

"Can't I?" His smile didn't falter.

And it made her acutely uncomfortable. Because she liked it. She wanted to curl up in its warmth like a cat in a sunbeam. "What do you really want, Mr. Cathcart?"

"Hamish," he insisted. "I thought we were friends."

Friends didn't kiss as if they were going up in flames in dark gardens.

But perhaps she was the only one who remembered that

incendiary kiss—Cathcart had more practical considerations upon his mind. "And I also thought we were associates. I've typeset the first few chapters, and brought them so you could see." He pulled his coat back enough to reveal a packet of printed sheets stuffed beneath his waistcoat. "And as your publisher, I have also come to pay you. Two hundred and fifty pounds. You left before we could settle things in a satisfactory manner."

She had, hadn't she? She had run home like the scared little field mouse she was, hiding herself in her country burrow. But he had followed her. How flattering. And troublesome. "You could have just left it with my Aunt Augusta."

"I tried—Lady Ivers confessed she didn't know if you were coming back either. So I set off to find out. And here I am."

"Elspeth! Why is he still here?"

Elspeth craned her neck to look over her shoulder at the ever-attentive aunts. "We can't discuss this here."

His smile widened, spreading that mischief around. "Well then, Miss Otis." His voice was warm with wicked amusement. "I can only hope you have a better, more private, place in mind."

Chapter 17

"MICHTY ME!" SHE blushed to the roots of her hair, a lovely shade of apricot. Like jam. Sweet and tart all at the same time.

Hamish knew he oughtn't let himself smile, but he was inordinately happy to have so easily found her. Happy to be watching her blush. Happy he had the power to make her blush.

"Elspeth? What's he saying?" the querulous old ladies in the tiny house queried.

"We're negotiating the price, mistress." Hamish raised his voice to carry into the cottage so the ladies didn't have to cup their hands around their ears. "She's a hard bargainer, your niece. Powerful hard. She's making this difficult for me."

The object of his negotiations kept her voice low so the old ladies might not hear. "Difficult? Nothing of the kind. You've only to take yourself right back to Edinburgh, where you belong. I'll send—"

He cut off her contingencies. "Oh, I don't intend to leave. At least not without you."

She stilled, one hand coming slowly to her throat, as if perhaps something he was saying was finally getting through to her. But then she shook it off. "I'm needed here."

"You're needed in Edinburgh, too. Or John Otis is, but

since you are, for my purposes, him, it will have to be you." He cast a glance at the two old crows perched at the wall. "Do they know?"

"About the books? Heaven forbid."

"Elspeth? Elspeth, what is he saying?"

She turned to Aunt Molly. "He's saying he'll do the thatch for a sovereign and a bowl of soup."

"Are you trying to swick me?" Hamish had to laugh at her audacity. "That's ridiculously low."

"Of course it is, Hamish. Of course. I'm *trying* to give you the perfect reason to refuse, since you can't possibly be anxious to thatch a roof."

"Actually, I am. Anxious to stay. Anxious to convince you. Anxious to find out all I can about you to use to my advantage." He was not surprised to find that he would do just about anything to remain near her, even manual labor. "I'm not going to give up that easily."

"You're mad—right off your big numpty head." She gaped at him. "Look at yourself. You're the son of an earl, even if you think you've rigged yourself in a lesser man's togs. You can't possibly be prepared to climb upon that wretchedly steep roof!"

"Don't fash yourself on my behalf, lass." He allowed himself the pleasure of playing his part. "I'm not so daft as to promise something I can't deliver." He would enlist the outdoor staff from Cathcart Lodge, his father's hunting box, just up the road, if need be. Whatever it took to remain. "I'll start with that trellis."

She shook her head, clearly flabbergasted at his ass-like stubbornness, and waved him out of the cottage. "Have it your way. But mind you don't ruin your coat."

THREE HOURS LATER, Hamish was sweaty, dirty, exasperated, and bloody from the thorns that had ripped his clothes and pierced his flesh with impunity. And very nearly regretting the impulse that had landed him in the briars. It had been an easy thing to think he would remain at Dove Cottage, as the charmingly ramshackle place was called, at all costs, until that cost became his blood.

Still, he had only to lay eyes upon her to know she was worth every difficulty and discomfort. She finally reappeared from the interior of the cottage looking harried and worn, as if those two old carrion crow aunts of hers had spent the intervening hours pecking away at her.

But she was bearing the promised bowl of steaming soup. And he was famished.

Who knew hard manual labor could be so invigorating? "Good evening, Miss Otis." He lifted his battered hat, though his sleeve was caught up in the rosebush's thorns. "I would offer you my arm, but this rosebush has insisted upon my escort until at least midnight."

He was rewarded by one of her quiet, small smiles, and he realized that she was tired—she had been working at least as hard as he. And she did it all day, every day, not just as a means to an end. This was her life here—one of constant servitude. Of constantly seeing to the needs of others before herself.

No wonder she had turned to writing with such imaginative romance. No wonder she had been so enthusiastic about the work in Edinburgh. It was as if she had been a butterfly let out of her chrysalis for a few days before she was shut back in, and made to be a caterpillar all over again.

Or perhaps her imagination worked as well here in the country as it did in Edinburgh. "Perhaps the rose is an enchanted fairy princess, who clings to keep you till midnight to break the awful spell and set her free." Her voice sounded wistful.

"And is that how you see yourself, the orphaned fairy princess forced to work for her crust of bread from her cruel aunts, laboring, fetching and carrying all the day through?"

"Goodness, nay." She shook her head and gave him a guarded smile, dismissing such an unflattering characterization. "Not a'tall. They are not cruel in the least—they are everything kind and forbearing, and have brought me up, and given me a home."

"And you take care of them in return." He would not argue with her version of events. "But what is to happen to you when they are gone—are you to live here all alone?"

The guarded warmth ebbed from her eyes. "I had not thought on it."

"Perhaps you should. I suppose you could write here as well as anywhere. Edinburgh isn't that far away. And if you were free to travel—" He stopped at the near-horrified look upon her face.

"I'll not be making plans over anyone's graves, Mr. Cathcart."

"No. I'm sorry. I didn't mean—" He was making a hash of it. "I only meant I feel certain that your aunt, Lady Ivers, would welcome you to come back to her in Edinburgh at any time, for any length of stay. In fact, she charged me with telling you her door is always open to you."

"That is very good of her, I'm sure. But I'm needed—"

"It is good of her," he confirmed. "And I must confess her wishes align with mine. I called at her house in St. Andrew Square, just as I said I would, Elspeth, for we had much to discuss. And not just about the books." He drank some of his soup so he wouldn't be tempted to reassure himself by stroking her pale cheek. "But you were gone."

"I had to come home. My aunt needed me. She still does, obviously."

"Yes, I see that. We all want something from you, don't we? But what matters more is what you really want."

She would not answer. "What is it *you* really want here, Hamish?"

"You," he said simply. "For you to come to Edinburgh and be happy and write me six more books just as scintillating and *romantic*—for that is the word we shall use in place of *erotic*, is it not— enough to pass the censure of the courts as the first."

More of that lovely apricot flush crept up the side of her

cheeks, as if she really were blushing at the word. "Are you trying on purpose to discommode me?"

"I am trying to entice and amuse you," he said instead, giving her one of his better, most hopeful smiles. "Is it working?"

"Perhaps." She pursed her lips, then crushed them between her teeth to keep the corners of her shy smile from turning up. "A little, perhaps."

"Enough to encourage you to do something for yourself? To leave your hidebound, little world?"

She shook her head more emphatically. "My world is neither hidebound nor small, Hamish. It is the same as everyone else's. Only not as…extensive or exciting. But it is *mine*."

She was right—she had not chosen her circumstances, but she did have to live with them. "Then perhaps I can be most helpful by expanding that world a little bit. Or at least make it more exciting."

She sighed and looked back at the listing cottage. "How are you going to do that?"

"By picking up where we left off. Do you know the last time you were kissed, Elspeth?"

She ducked her head. "At exactly fourteen minutes after eleven o'clock on Tuesday evening last."

"An eternity, " he assured her. "You were wearing blue."

"You were wearing a smile."

His need struck him like a heavy wave. He battered it back behind a dam of determination and restraint—damn flimsy materials on the best of days, but entirely permeable under the onslaught of this clever, sweet lass who looked like an angel, and left him in a hell of wanting.

"Just one kiss," he coaxed. "Just one."

"Elspeth? Where have you—" The older of the two crows appeared at the door. Her mouth pinched down to a beak of disapproval. "Come way from there, Elspeth. You're needed inside."

"Yes, Aunt Molly." She spared a last look over her shoulder. "Goodnight, sir."

"Goodnight, Miss Otis." He gifted her with a reassuring smile.

He would be her dear sir. He would win her yet.

Chapter 18

HAMISH WAS ALREADY quietly at work, unloading a wagonload of bundled straw for the thatching when Elspeth slipped out of the house as the early summer dawn lit the house with the first rays of sunlight.

"Where did you go last night?" she asked by way of greeting. The question had kept her up all night, tossing and turning in her narrow but comfortable bed. She hated to think of him sleeping under a damp hedgerow like a tramp, but the Aunts had forbidden her from offering him shelter within the cottage, and even overruled his sleeping in the empty shed.

"Miss Otis." He tipped his slouchy hat, and searched behind her for her minders.

"You needn't," she assured him, though she did so in a whisper. "They're not yet risen."

"In that case, good morning, Elspeth." He kept his voice low anyway, and reached out to capture her hand, bringing it to his lips. "I snuck off to Cathcart Lodge a few miles up the road." He pointed to the northwest. "Do you know it? The staff know me, and are prepared to keep quiet in exchange for a small consideration, which also covers Fergus there"—he indicated the man high upon Dove Cottage's roof—"managing the actual thatching while I assist. So, not to worry—I had a soft, clean bed."

As little as she had liked the thought of his sleeping in the hedgerow, she wasn't sure she ought to think of him in a soft, clean bed, either. Because his appearance—all opened collar and rolled up shirtsleeves—treated her to an absolutely spectacular version of Hamish Cathcart that was decidedly unlike the polished town gentleman she had encountered in Edinburgh. This morning he was all earthy manliness and competence as he tossed the bundled yelms of straw onto the roof. The muscles of his arm flexed and glistened in the rosy sunlight, and she—

"Elspeth? Elspeth, are you all to rights? Did you not get a good night's sleep?"

She had not, what with all the tossing and turning and wondering and wishing. But that was beside the point. Elspeth tethered her brain back to the present. "Are you really going to patch the thatch yourself?"

He smiled away her concern. "Aye." He settled a yelm of rolled straw onto his back and climbed up the rickety ladder as if he did it every day. "I'm a third son, Elspeth, not a pampered heir. I've brought along Fergus to manage the business so there are no mistakes, but I'm competent enough. With any luck, we'll be done before your Aunts even know we're up there."

An eminently practical plan. Elspeth had to admire his forethought in arranging things so neatly—amongst other things she admired, like his long, lean legs encased in leather breeches, his strong, well-formed shoulders, and his rangy, tapered back.

But she knew better than most not to judge a person on appearance alone. With Hamish, there was also his clever, amusing mind—a potent, knee-weakening combination.

Elspeth firmed her knees and shaded her eyes to gaze up at him, this handsome, amusing man. Whom she had thought of all the night through. "May I help, too?"

He eyed her browned arms, and Elspeth could not keep herself from curling her calloused hands into fists to keep herself from feeling coarse and countrified.

"No perfumed miss, you," he observed.

"No." Elspeth tried to push aside the constant shadow of her self-doubt—they were not in a gilded mansion now, and he'd likely want calluses of his own after thatching the roof. "Aye, although I will have you know I do use perfumed soap."

"Aye. Verbena."

Heat rose from somewhere beneath her stays when she realized the intimacy of his observation, warming her more thoroughly than the rising sun. "Aye." She had distilled the scent from the flowers in the garden, and made the soap herself.

"I suppose you could help, at that," he agreed, as if he were doing her the grandest of favors. "You could pass the rest of those bundles up to me—the yelms aren't heavy."

Elspeth set herself to the task, mostly because it was the sensible thing to do—if he saw the roof repaired quickly, the Aunts might be better inclined toward him. But also because she liked this heady mixture of excitement and longing that stirred her up insides in his presence. She liked the tart pleasure of sparring with him so pleasantly.

She would miss that when he was gone.

She *had* missed it terribly, when she'd come running home, only to find Aunt Isla not nearly as ill as expected, and only taking a turn for the worse whenever a return to Edinburgh was mentioned. But what could she do? She couldn't leave.

But perhaps he could stay?

And so, once all the bundles of straw had been passed up to him, Elspeth amused them both by scrambling nimbly onto the roof and continuing to make herself useful, twisting up the hazel sticks used to anchor the stacked straw thatch. She'd attempted to patch the thinning roof a time or two herself, and a miserable, difficult job it had been. But working together with Hamish and his man Fergus in companionable silence, the three of them were able to make the repairs in less than half the time it might otherwise have taken.

A feeling of contentment washed over her like a balm— it was always a lovely thing to complete a task well done, and a lovelier thing to know that her aunts' roof was now sturdy enough to withstand next winter's rains.

His work done, Fergus climbed down from the roof, but Elspeth was loath to return to earth where she would have to take up the grave weight of care that pinned her to this patch of Scottish soil once more. Up on the roof, the summer sky boded clear and fair. The countryside was waking to a new day. The orchard was filling with birdsong and the hedgerows were bustling with unseen animal comings and goings It was all as familiar and comfortable as her old, green country cloak.

Then why then did she miss the noisy hustle and dirty bustle of Auld Reeky?

Because that was where Hamish would be soon.

But he was here now, with her, on a roof, looking like something out of her narrow dreams—rugged and rumpled and manly with his sleeves rolled back to expose his forearms. Looking forbidden and wished-for all at the same time. Looking like forever.

Elspeth leaned her elbows back against the stiff prickle of the thatch, and made herself look away from him and his intriguing forearms. Over the trees and rooftops, the land stretched away in a hundred different tumbled shades of green. "It's almost as if you can see the whole of the world beyond the village from up here."

Hamish put a bit of straw between his teeth, and looked to the east. "Can you see as far as Edinburgh?"

"No," she sighed and changed the direction of her gaze northward, orienting herself by the hulking comfort of the Pennine Hills. "I can't let my gaze reach quite that far."

"Or your ambitions?" he asked quietly, casually shading his eyes from the sharp slanted ray of the morning sun, as if he had no vested interest in the answer. As if it were not the whole of the reason he had come to find her.

"Perhaps," she answered truthfully, for once not trying to evade the real subject that lay between them like a fish on the bank of a burn, gasping for water. The truth was she wanted both worlds—she wanted to be able to take care of the Aunts, to repay in kind the sacrifices they had made for her. But she also wanted to write and to be with Hamish. To talk to him of books and lessons in kissing, and feel beautiful and clever and brilliant and capable of genius again. "I have been writing," she confessed. "Or rather rewriting *A Memoir of a Game Girl*—secretly, of course."

She had stuffed rags beneath her attic door so the Aunts couldn't hear the telltale scratch of the pen against the foolscap or see the light from her candle stubs as she worked into the night.

Hamish rolled toward her, onto his side, so he could search her face. "For myself and Prufrock, I'm glad to hear it. But you don't look glad—you look tired."

As much as it might mortify her, Elspeth had a mirror, and knew it for the truth. "I am tired," she admitted. "But not so tired or awful as I would feel if they found out."

"Would it be so bad?" He frowned in contemplation. "Perhaps you underestimate them?"

"Oh, no—they'd be horrified." She was sure of it. And she was just as sure that she didn't want to horrify them. The Aunts Murray might be strict and fussy and not nearly as much fun as Aunt Augusta, but they were her family. And they needed her now, the same way she had needed them as a child. Her absence had more than discommoded them— Isla had made herself ill with worry.

"Elspeth? Elspeth!" It was as if the mere *thought* of the Aunts had conjured them out of the cottage.

Elspeth knew she ought to call down and tell them where she was. But she didn't. Because that would be the end of contentment and ease—the end of closeness and harmony.

So she raised her finger to her lips to signal Hamish to silence, flattened herself against the thatch, and waited until the Aunts' fussy murmurings faded slowly into the morning's silence.

"I'm trying to understand." He reached idly for her work-roughened hand. "Clearly you're not entirely happy and easy here—why would you not want to be free to return to Edinburgh with me?"

Because as much as she wanted to go, she could not bear to leave the Aunts behind. And Elspeth was sure he did not mean the invitation in the same way her foolish heart had instantly taken it—literally. It was like a fever dream, the idea that she could go back to Edinburgh with him, and be with him always. In real life, earls' sons did not marry scandalous writers' bastard daughters.

For despite Aunt Augusta's kind claim to the contrary, the sisters Murray had explained that there was simply no evidence—no documents or witnesses—to prove that her parents had ever been married. Elspeth was as she had always been—illegitimate. And *that,* more than the caps or the quiet life in a forgotten village, was what made her an un-marriageable spinster.

For her foolish heart's sake, she must accept the inevitable. "Hamish—"

He must have heard the excuse in her voice. "But what of us? And the books. And your Aunt Augusta." He lowered his voice. "And what about kissing?" He drew her hand to his mouth, and suited words to deed, brushing her knuckles against his lips. "I don't think you understand how extraordinary it is—our compatibility. Our mutual attraction. At least I hope it's mutual."

Elspeth felt the scorching heat of that attraction burn up her cheeks and sweep to the roots of her hair. Oh, to kiss him again. To feel wanted and desirable. To feel such pleasure. But then where would she be?

Rolling about a roof with a man who could not marry her.

But so what if she were?

If her Aunts were right, and no one was to marry her on account of her birth, why should she not have this one shining moment with him—with Hamish.

She wouldn't think and worry and retreat—she would do. Just as she had the morning when she had taken her heart in her hands and set off for Edinburgh.

Just as she would now.

Without another word, Elspeth simply pulled herself close and pressed her lips to his. She wrapped her arms about his neck and clung to him—clung to the warmth and ease and happiness she felt in his arms. Clung to the fragile hope that this moment would be enough to last a lifetime. That his kiss would warm her through of all the lonely cold nights to come.

She slanted her lips across his, angling to get close, and closer still. His arms came around the small of her back as if he knew what she wanted—the weight and press of his rangy strength tethering her to the sun-warmed cushion of thatch. As if he knew just what to do to silence all of her inner objections.

His hand curled around her nape and tangled in her hair, disrupting the neat pins, arcing her head back to deepen their kiss, and deepen the arching intimacy of the moment alone on top of the world.

She made the most of it—her hands were in his hair, too, fisting up the unruly brown curls. Everything was feeling and sensuality—every taste, every smell, every texture was amplified—his body all against the length of her, every nerve and sinew alive to the power and delight.

She arched against him, giving herself over to the moment. To the hope of lasting pleasure. There were years of longing and wanting and not being good enough in her kiss. Years to go of wanting and missing him yet.

But up there on the roof, in the light and sun and air, as if she were above the earth above all the problems and insurmountable decisions and endless concerns. The breeze was fresher, the sun was warmer, the scent of the thatch was sweeter, and the precious seconds stretched longer so she could abide with him and let the rest of the world slip away.

But they were slipping, too—sliding a few frightening inches down the smooth slant of thatch.

She gasped into his kiss, but Hamish was himself, and laughed and said, "I've got you," and kissed her some more.

And he did indeed have her—she was still safely held in his arms in the fragrant cradle of thatch, being loved. "Oh, Hamish. I wish this could be every day. I wish I wasn't—"

She didn't finish the sentence, and he didn't try to finish it for her. Not with words, anyway. But he kissed her with a different sort of feeling—with a hesitation, a tender urgency, it seemed, as if he were already accepting that they must part.

He lifted his head and framed her face with his hands, as if wanted to memorize her. As if he knew it could not last. "We should probably not tempt fate any longer."

"No," she agreed though her heart and her hands cried out the opposite.

When he eased off of her, she could not keep herself from grasping his hand to kiss one last time before he pulled away. Before he pulled away. Before he inevitably left her.

That was when she heard it—the distant toll of the kirk bell calling the village to worship. Tolling her name like a sentence. Or a curse.

"Oh, no." Elspeth felt all the last of her comfort and ease drain away, to be replaced with cold, sickening dread. "Oh, Hamish, I'd completely forgotten it was Sunday."

Chapter 19

NEVER HAVING BEEN much of a kirk-going sort of fellow, Hamish didn't share her dread, but he did understand family obligations. "I shouldn't have kept you. But I won't regret it. Not for a moment." He was also a realist. "Does this mean the harridans are gone?"

"They're not harridans," she answered hotly. "They're my family."

As his own family was more often a burden than a blessing, Hamish's view of the matter was decidedly more cynical than Elspeth's. "But that means we have more time together."

"I don't know." She looked in the direction of the kirk and bit her lip in agitation, as if she were not sure if she did not already regret the passionate interlude on the roof. "Perhaps I ought to go on now, even though I'm going to be intolerably late."

Having been late to chapel at Castle Cathcart a time or twelve in his youth, Hamish could readily imagine the scene that would greet her if she did so—the disapproving silence coupled with pointed, probing stares. The terrible judgment.

He would spare Elspeth that, if he could. "Why don't we make the most of the moment? It's a perfect morning for fishing, and we can make up for the sin of missing kirk by getting fresh fish for breakfast."

"Oh, I don't know, Hamish," she havered. "This is already a disaster."

"Only if you let it be." He did not wait for her to agree, but seized the day, and took her by the hand. "Come. I saw some old fishing tackle in your shed that I'm sure will do the trick. Come with me to the burn and I'll teach you how to fish."

"There's a trick to catching fish?"

"Oh, aye. Fear not, I'll teach you everything you need to know," he promised, lest she be put off. "You won't even have to get your feet wet."

She finally put aside whatever other objections she might have had, and allowed him the pleasure of taking her by the hand, and leading her down the ladder to the shed, and following him along the rocky burn to a still pool, from whence he might instruct her.

"We'll start with the grip. Thumb on top, like so." It was all a ruse, the instruction, so he might have her nearer, in his arms again. He came close behind her, making a welcoming cover of his body to shelter her, to demonstrate the motion of casting. And to inhale the soothing scent of her skin. She smelled of the garden she tended so meticulously—of lemon, verbena, and mint. Of sunshine and warmth on such a blessedly bright summer morning.

He positioned himself as close against her back as instruction, if not good sense, allowed. "You'll want to hold it thusly, Elspeth."

Her smile was as shy and luminous as it had been the first time he had seen her in Fowl's Close. "Thank you, Hamish. I'll see if I can muster…"

"A firm wrist," he advised, "you'll want to bend the rod, and sling the line like…"—he demonstrated proper motion—"this."

The line cast somewhat heavily into the pool on the far side of the burn, but he accomplished his goal—she was nodding, looking suitably impressed with his casting prowess. Which allowed him to move on to the next lesson.

His first kiss he placed at the side of her neck, just above the collarbone, where her skin was soft and fine and sensitive. He nipped lightly, kissing his way up to her jaw. Her head fell gently to the side, silently acquiescing to his plans for a different sort of demonstration than mere fishing.

In fact, all thought of fishing was forgotten when she arched back to meet his lips with hers. He angled his head to gently suck her bottom lip until she opened her mouth to him, unfurling like a spring flower, soft and sweet. So sweet he was unprepared for her to turn within his arms, fitting herself flush against him, kissing him back, tasting him with hungry little nips and tentatively questing tongue. His chest expanded with heat and need and a desperation to keep her by his side, in his arms. To convince her that she ought to come with him.

His arms tightened around her, pulling her closer still, drawing her down into deeper intimacy. "Darling lass," he encouraged. "How can you want to stay here when you could have kisses always?"

She stilled, her hands going taut on his shoulders. "Always?"

"Aye. I would come to your Aunt Augusta's house every day so we could work on the book together." The idea was like an intoxicant. With the completion of the second book he would be assured of success. He would be free of his father's threats, free to choose as he pleased. "Think of it, Elspeth. We could—"

But she did not want to hear his plans and possibilities. She turned away, slowly shaking her head. "Hamish. What you want is impossible for me."

He refused to hear it. "It is not impossible. It is the easiest thing. All we have to do is return to Edinburgh."

"Away from all this." She shook her head, and said nothing more, while she picked up the abandoned fishing rod. "I'd best get us breakfast."

Hamish was about to instruct her on how to gather the line, but the damned clever lass looped her line and let loose an effortlessly flawless cast that landed like the merest breath of a breeze on the surface of the dark, glassy water, and with one subtle draw, she had a fish on the hook and was smoothly reeling it in.

Humility—an emotion he rarely felt—tipped him right off his rock pedestal and into the ankle-deep water. "Well, damn me for an ass. You're nothing short of an expert, you faker."

"I never had to pretend, Hamish. You were too busy instructing and being clever to think—I'm a country lass who's lived along this burn all my life."

He waded his way to the bank to dry out, contemplate the beauty of the morning and the graceful strength of her casts, which were so quietly efficient, it was only a matter of an hour's work of a dozen unhurried casts before she had put another two fish in the creel.

"Is there nothing you can't do?" he asked with all seriousness. "Write books, care for ungrateful auld ladies, thatch roofs, catch fish?"

"They're not ungrateful, she objected. "But I can't make satisfactory jam." Her smile was a little sad and bittersweet. "The Aunts say I haven't the patience."

"Ballocks." He was instantly ready to defend her against the pecking of the crows. "You've exhibited a fine amount of patience with me, and even more patience and finesse with that fly rod."

She sighed but shook her head. "Flattery will get you everywhere."

"Will it? Will it get you to Edinburgh?"

"Hamish." Her answer was only slightly more forthcoming than silence, but just as chiding. She looked up at the morning sky and the sun rising high overhead, as if only just realizing what time it must be getting on to be "Has it gone as late as that? I really ought to get back—the Aunts will wonder and worry even more if I am not there when they get back from kirk."

He curbed his instinct to talk her into staying and shirking her duties, and, instead, walked her back to the orchard gate. "Even if you are late, you'll bring them a tasty breakfast."

"I will. But here"—she scooped one of the trout out of

the wicker creel, and handed it to him—"You'll need one for your breakfast as well."

"I do, thank you." He tried to prolong the contact as long as he might—made sure to brush his hand along her wrist, and his fingers lingered just long enough so she might understand the pleasure he took from her touch. "I won't try and keep you. I know I told you I would go today, but there is still work that could be done. I could have a go at shoring up those rotting eaves. The timbers—"

"Hamish. Please." She looked up at him with the whole of her soul shining in her clear blue eyes. "Please don't ask for things that are not in my power to give."

Chapter 20

DISAPPROVAL HUNG AS thick as the scent from the rose vine outside the garden door by the time Elspeth made it home. Even at a run, she had arrived home well after the Aunts had already returned from the village kirk.

"We missed you at services, Elspeth," Aunt Molly began in a voice laden with reproach.

"I am sorry." And Elspeth was, deeply so. She had not missed a Sunday service—barring illness, which had only happened once, when she had come down with a fever—in all the twenty odd years she had lived with her Aunts at Dove Cottage. "I woke early and thought it was a fine day for the thatching, and once we got working, I seem to have lost track of the time. Though the roof is well finished and very stout now, so you'll have no worries it will leak come winter."

"The work might have waited on a Sunday, Elspeth," Aunt Molly chided. "What has come over you? It isn't like you to miss something as important as divine services."

"Yes, Aunt. I am truly sorry." There was really nothing else Elspeth could say.

But she would not regret her morning. She would not allow anything to dim her memory of her last few hours with him. What a lovely going away present those last golden hours had been.

"I'll just get your breakfast eggs started on the boil." She headed for the kitchen fireplace.

Aunt Molly stepped into the doorway, blocking her way. "Where did you get that creel?" Her aunt turned toward the garden, almost as if she could see through the worn bricks and boards to the dusty collection of auld fishing gear in the shed. "It's been years since we've had any new fishing equipment here."

"No." Elspeth swallowed the dry apprehension in her mouth, but gave them the honest truth. "It's not new. I just dusted it off so we—"

"We?"

"No. I mean, I caught the fish. For you. For breakfast, since I missed kirk, and I—"

But Aunt Molly had not been born yesterday, nor even the day after. "Elspeth Otis." She looked at Elspeth over the top of her spectacles. "Your neck is going all pink." She had always been able to detect even the flimsiest fib when Elspeth had been a child. "Were you with that tramp?"

"He's not a tramp—he's a gentleman. I met him in Edinburgh," she admitted.

"Edinburgh?" Aunt Molly still did not comprehend. "If he's a gentleman, what was he doing in our roses and on our roof?"

Elspeth gave up all prevarication. "Because he has come here, to Dove Cottage, to find me." Even in the midst of being caught lying, she took a sort of perverse pride and pleasure in that knowledge. "He was only pretending to be a gardener."

"Pretending?" Aunt Molly's hand rose to her throat, as if the word itself were poison.

"Yes, Aunt. Because he's not really a gardener or a thatcher." Because Elspeth was tired of pretending, too. "He's a publisher of books. And he's publishing my book, or rather my father's book." She corrected her presumption, but the subtle difference was lost upon the Aunts who stared at her as if she had finally run irretrievably mad.

It was Aunt Molly who finally spoke. "I refuse to believe

it."

It was such a simple, little word, refuse, but it hit Elspeth with the force of twenty years of denial. Twenty years of holding back. Twenty years of being called, "Elspeth!" in that disparaging tone, of not being legitimate, of never being thought good enough.

"Refuse all you like. It's my legacy from my father, my fortune, those books. And I refuse to listen to you disparage him any more. I won't hear another word against him "

"Nay," Aunt Molly swore, as if she could deny Elspeth any such legacy. "There is nothing you need from such a man. Have we not given you everything you need? Have we not given you a home and made you feel welcome?"

"Nay." It was Elspeth's turn to deny the charge. "You have. But—"

"It's that devil's cub, Augusta Ivers, who's turned your head, and turned you against us."

"Nay!" Elspeth wouldn't hear of it. "Aunt Augusta was everything kind and encouraging—"

"Encouraging you to consort with strange men!"

Elspeth prayed for patience. "Not consorting, Aunt. Contracting—working with him the same as any author." If one kissed every author one contracted, and thatched their roof and fished for their breakfast in the morning sunshine.

"Have you lain with him?"

The blunt question felt more like an accusation. "Nay! How could you ask such a thing?"

Her voice was hot and tight and scratchy with the pain— the pain of knowing she was breaking their frail old hearts as well as her own.

"You've changed since you went away, Elspeth. We hardly know you anymore."

She hardly knew herself anymore. Perhaps she never had. But it was past time.

"Perhaps I have." She firmed her voice, refusing to be cowed—refusing to regret. "Perhaps I'm not afraid of changing. Perhaps I want to be transformed."

She *had* wanted it, with all her soul.

"That huzzy encouraged you, no doubt." Isla finally said her piece.

Hurt and anger banked for twenty years lent Elspeth's voice righteous heat. "Speak of me how you will—how you always have, as if I'm not good enough. But you leave Lady Augusta Ivers out of it. She has been nothing but kind and generous and thoughtful—"

"And I suppose we haven't?" Aunt Molly's voice was becoming shrill.

Even through the hot sting of the tears burning her eyes, Elspeth tried to stay calm, tried to listen and modulate her own voice, even as her anger made her voice shake. "That's not what I said."

"You've said quite enough, Elspeth Otis." Aunt Molly's tone was as emphatic as it was feeble. "Quite enough."

"Blood will out, I've always said," Isla said, as she clutched her sister's hand for support.

"Aye," Molly sniffed. "And I'm afraid to say it's true."

There was nothing more Elspeth could say. Nothing more that she wouldn't regret.

She was so tired of being *not enough*. Of working so hard to be something she was not. She didn't want to be sweet and polite and obedient and do as she ought anymore. She wanted to *live*.

Blood would out, they said. Well, perhaps it was time to make it so.

Chapter 21

ELSPETH RAN—HER feet seemed to know what to do better than her heart. She ran after him, heading back the way she had just come, racing through the orchard trying to catch him before he disappeared forever.

He had said the Cathcart hunting lodge lay a few miles to the northwest, so she headed that way, running as fast as her legs would carry her, and there he was, just passing the last of the gnarled apple trees on the far side of the orchard.

"Hamish!"

He stopped and turned back at her call. "Elspeth. I thought—"

She threw herself at him as soon as she reached him, jumping into his arms and looping her arms around his neck in the most forward manner. But she couldn't seem to help herself. She needed the support of his arms immediately coming round her back to hold her close. She wanted the comfort of his surprised murmur. "What's all this?"

"I've done it." She mustered her wits, and pulled herself out of his arms. "I've kicked over the traces." And she was glad of it. "Gone over the hedge."

"Which particular hedge, Elspeth? There are so many to choose from."

"My aunts' hedge. I've told them all." The words tumbled

over each other in her rush to get them out. "I've told them that I wrote the book, and that you are publishing it, and that I'm going to go to Edinburgh with you, and that I love you."

The sentiment came as no less of a shock to Elspeth than it could be to Hamish—she had not said such a thing to her Aunts, but now that she had made the declaration, she knew it for the truth, and did not wish it unsaid. "I do."

"Elspeth." He met her admission with a kiss that soothed every agitation and was a balm to every concern. "Ye gods, Elspeth."

She reached for him, pulling his mouth down to hers, and everything else melted away but the persuasive pressure of his lips against hers, his arms holding her tight, his body pressed close and warm. She turned her head, angling to get closer, to deepen the kiss.

His hands cradled her face, holding her still as his tongue swept across the lips and into her mouth, and his kiss was everything he was—strong and confident and hedonistic and raw—and it made her want to be those things. To be as strong and confident in her love—to be his equal in this as in all other things.

She opened to him, to the startling sensations that careered through her body, back and forth from her lips to her breasts, making them feel needy and tight. The hurt and resentment that sent her running to him began to give way to desire—deep in her belly the ache she felt as if she had carried forever began to ease, the agitation giving way to pleasure.

She let him bear her down into the soft fragrant grass, and he was on her, around her, pulling her into his heat and shelter. She held tight to his shirt front, anchoring herself to him—to the only thing still real in her world. The weight of his body pressed her hands between them, and she loosened her grip on his shirt, only to find her hands flat against the solid shape of his torso. Her fingers began to roam of their own accord, up across his collar and along the breadth of his shoulders, out along the sculpted curve of his upper arms, down across the taut flat of his belly.

He made a sound that was equal parts frustration and

encouragement, and he ducked his head to kiss and worry at the side of her neck, nosing and nipping until she turned her head to grant him greater access.

And she wanted greater access, too—she fisted up his shirttails so she could slide her hands beneath the rough linen, and set her palms flat against the sleek plane of his back, and feel the heat of his skin.

He let out a fervent sound of near-pain, and almost sprang back from her, kneeling above her to rip off the waistcoat and shirt and fling them away unseen. He closed his eyes when she put her hands back to his bared skin, hissing a breath in through his teeth—a pleased rather than painful sound.

She did it again, stroking across his smooth flesh, and he swore roughly under his breath, and collapsed down onto her, pinning her hands flat to his nipples with his weight.

He lay upon her for only a moment before he levered himself away, and went at the laces of her sturdy quilted jumps with a speed approaching haste, as if he were untying a Christmas present to himself. But no sooner were the laces ripped away and the quilted over-stays flung to join his waistcoat on some lower branch, than he loosed the drawstring of her modest shirt, and was pushing it away with the straps of her lightly-boned stays and chemise to bare her shoulders.

Beneath the confines of the remaining layers, her breasts began to feel full and aching. One hand rounded to her back, and she arched toward him to give him access, her nipples contracting and rasping with painful pleasure against the starched muslin of her stays.

His mouth returned to hers, the rough, taut texture of his lips rubbing against hers, the whisky-laced tang of his tongue tangling with hers as he kissed and kissed and kissed her.

And she was kissing him back, returning his heated, open-mouthed kisses with all the fervor she had kept hidden under the tight lashing across her soul, urging him with her lips to rid her of all traces of clothing until she was as bare as he.

This was the mad pleasure she had tried to write about—this was the intoxicating rush of sensation she had only given expression in words put finally into glorious deed.

And then her blouse and stays and chemise gave way to this hands, and he bared her to the waist, revealing the tight furls of her breasts, aching and sensitive in the cool morning air. His hands closed over them carefully, caressing, worshiping. He dragged his thumbs across the peaks, and feeling and sound blossomed out of her—a gasp that matched the exquisite and unexpected bliss—and she pushed herself up into his hands, letting her head fall back, closing her eyes so she could only feel. Only feel him. And the pleasure that grew like a rose out of the thorns of her life.

He followed his hands with his mouth, closing his lips around one sensitive nipple, licking and sucking at her, sending seeds of want and need falling to ground deep in her belly.

A sound of shocked surprise blossomed from her mouth, and Elspeth opened her eyes to the glorious green daylight, opening her soul to the sensations snaking through her body, the tight tension that twined through her like a vine, clinging and coiling deep. She wanted to move with it, to twist and turn against him. Her fingers curled into his hair, holding his head as her body undulated like a flower bent by the strong summer wind.

"Aye, lass," he breathed against her skin. "That's the way of it." Encouraging her with his words, filling her with something more desperate than anticipation as he kneed her legs apart and settled himself hard against the juncture of her thighs. His lips returned to hers as his body joined hers in movement, creating a dance to music that they alone could hear—the strings of nature's symphony, the song of the skylark and the keening cry of the hawk.

His work-roughened hands fell to her skirts, dragging up the hem, exposing her legs to the bright summer air. And then his hands were back at her breasts, fondling and fawning until heat and something fiercer, something bright and shining and insistent, budded to life within, pulsing up from her belly. Between her thighs, her muscles clenched in heightened anticipation.

Finally, she was going to do exactly what she wanted.

Chapter 21

"ELSPETH. SWEET, SWEET Elspeth." His voice was shredded, wisps of grass blown and bent, as he rucked up her skirts. "Are you sure?"

She followed his gaze down the length of their bodies to the pale tangle of curls at the apex of her thighs. Her body seemed to shift within itself, changing into something new and different, uncharted ground in the small map of her life.

"Aye," she said, more to herself, as well as him. She was sure of herself. And sure of him.

She wanted to say yes to new and different, yes to change. Yes to the new dance between their bodies—a dance that quickened with the possessive touch of his hands on the bared flesh of her upper thighs.

"Aye," he echoed, lowering his forehead to rest against hers.

Between their bodies, she felt him touch and part her vulnerable flesh. But she didn't feel vulnerable—she felt open and strong and proud when he touched her. Her muscles clenched in delight, her skin came alive with sensation, streaking across the surface. And she was arching up into his hand, like a blossom seeking the warmth of the sun, needing to be closer and closer still.

"Elspeth."

His call came like a prayer to her ears, a plea that only she could hear, a boon only she could grant. "Aye," she answered, assenting to whatever he might ask, wanting anything of this heavy delight drenching her in bliss.

He slid one long finger inside her, and a ripple of strong pleasure surged through her, radiating outward, growing stronger and stronger, until it was a wave of sensation that crashed through her, making her gasp for air.

"Sweet Elspeth," he crooned against her ear as he worked his other hand beneath to cup her bottom.

She arched into the aching bliss as he took the tight, needy peak of her breast back between his lips, and she made another inarticulate sound of pleasure and want and abandon, giving herself over to the exquisite torture of pleasure.

His breath answered, harsh and strained at her ear. "Let me love you. Let me lie with you."

His words elicited something so sharp and so strong and so near to hurt it was as if the need was clawing its way out of her soul. "Aye, Hamish. Love me. Lie with me. Please."

His head swooped down and captured the nubbin of her straining nipple, teasing it with his teeth before sucking fiercely, as he loosened the fall of his breeks and positioned himself at the opening of her body.

She could hear and feel the rasp of his breath coming in audible pants, as if breathing had begun to pain him. As if the need within him was just as sharp and cutting. She planted her feet flat against the carpet of grass, pushing herself into his weight, bucking her hips against the strong probe of his rod beneath the covering of his breeches.

Now it was he who made an inarticulate, animal sound of pleasure as he worked himself free, shoving interfering clothing away so they could be flesh to flesh. Skin to naked skin. Heart to open heart. "Elspeth, I need—"

She needed, too. She wanted. She ached to be one with him.

She went at the loosened folds of his clothes, pushing the fine, rumpled linen of his shirt over his head, using her toes and feet to shuck his breeks from his sleek flanks so she could wrap her arms around his bare back and grasp the strong pillar of his neck.

And still she needed more. She needed the push of his body into hers. She needed the strength of his hands gripping her hips, pulling her tight to him as he bore down into her body, until he was inside her and around her, filling the emptiness within with his body and his love.

There was a tight moment of uncomfortable friction, but it dissolved, dissipating into something sweet and yearning. Something that built, piling up like a hayrick, loose and billowing. And then he began to move and the pleasure was shifting, raining down around her, falling apart and blowing away to leave the want open and exposed.

She felt as if she were being ridden on the wind, racing faster and faster toward some steeple over the next hill, and she couldn't breathe for the pace. Couldn't hear or speak or think. Couldn't do anything but abandon herself to his driving rhythm, riding the pleasure higher and higher up the hill.

She could hear the gasps he drew from her as he rode faster still, giving way to abandonment with each increasingly mindless stroke of his body into hers.

"Please," she heard, and had no idea whether it was he or she that spoke.

But he answered by grasping her bottom with both his hands, holding her hips, tilting them upward to meet his strokes.

She wrapped her legs around him, grasping him tight to her, straining to hold the reins.

He arched up on his knees, a growling howl of pleasure and need and anguished triumph tunneling out of his chest. She felt it vibrate all the way through her, bringing her pleasure and pain and joy that she had to touch his face, had to make him open his eyes to see her. To see how much she loved him.

She reached out to stroke his face, and he turned into her caress, kissing and nipping at her fingers. He smiled down at her, his beautiful body moving above her, dancing just for her, until she could no longer meet the heat in his eyes, and closed her own against the tide of feeling that surged within, drenching and tumbling all at the same time.

He cried out, pulsing into her so strongly her climax broke over her like a wave of flame, taking her up and burning her to a glowing cinder spiraling away, upward into the sky.

<h1 style="text-align:center">Chapter 23</h1>

HAMISH CAME BACK to himself slowly, as if he had taken a clout to the head and was still in a daze. He rolled onto his back on the thick grass and gathered Elspeth to him. His Elspeth, who lifted her sweet face to the sunshine like a pagan worshiper.

He felt rather pagan himself after having worshiped her with his body—awed and honored and beyond thrilled that she had chosen him to gift with her body. Because he wasn't remotely worthy

But he would make himself be—he would rise to the occasion.

What a fool he had been to think that only experience conferred wisdom. What an ass he had been to overlook the strength of innocence. Elspeth was his ideal because she was both, and neither.

Upon that particularly impractical and philosophically convoluted thought, Hamish took her hand, lacing their fingers together, holding her in quiet, simple intimacy. It felt good and right and wonderful and terrifying.

Because he wanted this feeling, this warm bubble of quiet contentment to last forever.

But it could not. Life had to go on. Decisions had to be made.

But not quite yet. Not until the heat of lust had ebbed enough to make her shy and wanting her clothes.

She turned her back to set herself to rights, and Hamish did the same, until they could stand before each other without blushing.

Hamish brushed a long strand of grass from her hair. "You'll come with me to the lodge? We can make plans there. Decide what needs to be done."

He would speak to her Aunts later. Declare himself as a gentleman ought.

The decision gave him a warm feeling of rightness. Or belonging—belonging to something, and someone, he had chosen for himself. Elspeth was the beginning of a family of his own, free from the encumbrances and expectations of his parents. Free from their guilt and hypocrisy. Free to write books and laze about orchards all day if they wanted.

"All right." She gave him a luminously hopeful smile. "Aye."

"It will all be right as rain, Elspeth," he assured her. "We'll be the happiest people in all of Scotland. In all of Britain."

"I already am."

He laced his fingers with hers and pulled her to standing. "I hope your Aunts won't tax me with not fixing their eaves today, but I find I have other, more pressing commitments."

Her smile was as luminous as the noonday sun. "Like me?"

"Exactly like you." They walked in companionable, contented silence along the dozing hedgerows until they reached the lane that led to Cathcart Lodge. But as soon as they stepped onto the grassy track, Hamish had to draw Elspeth back, into the verge when a four in hand coach sped close by, forcing them to crowd into the hedgerow to let it safely pass.

But immediately after it did, a familiar face popped out of the window, and the coach began to slow, coming to a full stop.

Ye gods.

Something that wasn't yet alarm sent a warning chill down

his spine.

He knew that face from Edinburgh. And that of the young, fashionably dressed lady, stepped lightly into the grassy lane. Master Lorrimer, a brewer from Edinburgh's southwest side, climbed down after his daughter and heir. Hamish had met them but once, at a shooting weekend, but he feared their intent.

"Mr. Cathcart?" Miss Lorrimer called. "Hamish!" She smiled and waved. "I thought that was you. I told Papa it was so."

Alarm shifted to suspicion that hit him like a shovel to the back of his head—Hamish could all but feel his father's hand stirring this pot.

"Elspeth, why don't you go on to the Lodge. I'll follow you directly."

But Elspeth had no time to respond before the brewer's daughter had made her way down the lane upon them. "Don't go, Hamish. It won't do you know, running away, looking like a scarecrow, with straw in your hair. Not when we've driven all this way to find you." She smiled in a way that bared her teeth, much like an aggressive dog, grinning before it bites. "Rusticating with dairy maids, have you been, Hamish? Your mother will be all agog to hear."

So perhaps not his father's hand. But still, his family was stirring the hot pot he seemed to have landed in. "Miss Lorrimer. You will excuse me, please." He would not introduce Elspeth, for such was the surest way to have her name spread about Edinburgh like a contagion.

"I will not, unless I have your promise that I shall meet with you dancing attendance upon me at the Marchioness of Queensbury's Masquerade ball in Edinburgh on Thursday next. I expect that will be the perfect evening to announce our betrothal, will it not?"

It would not. But her words had already hit Elspeth like a hard slap to the face—he could see her head snap back with the force of the lie. "Betrothal?"

"No. It's not like that," Hamish began.

"The devil you say!" The brewer himself stepped forward

like a guard dog at his daughter's side.

Miss Lorrimer's laughing expression stilled, and became serious. "Your family, not to mention the solicitors, say differently, Mr. Cathcart, along with my Papa."

"Aye," Master Lorrimer growled. "Beggin' your pardon, sir, but I do." The man was polite but emphatic. "Signed the papers this morning, Mr. Cathcart. I was given to believe you'd be there to make things all right and tight, and when you weren't, why I set out for to find you straightaway. And here we are."

Here they all were. Except for Elspeth, who had already turned tail, and, very sensibly, run away from this fine madness.

Would that Hamish could do the same.

But he could not. He would not. He would face the fire and extinguish it.

Chapter 24

ELSPETH DID WHAT she had always been taught to do—make herself so small and quiet that she erased herself from the conversation. But this time, she could not simply retreat to the privacy of her imagination. This time, she had to run to escape the sharp eyes of Hamish's betrothed, Miss Lorrimer, who had looking her over as if Elspeth were the veriest slattern.

Where she ran was a matter of indifference. Through the trees, along the river and deep into the shadow of the woods was all she could think, letting the branches claw at her skirts and switch at her skin, running onward until her lungs were burning with shame and fury and she collapsed onto her knees, and lay sobbing in the moss-covered bracken.

She sobbed out the ache in her chest until it gradually grew smaller and smaller, hardening into something small enough to manage. Small enough to swallow.

Hamish's betrothed.

She looked the part, Miss Lorrimer did—well dressed and well spoken, as if she would belong in Edinburgh, or Cathcart Lodge or the Marchioness of Queensbury's Masquerade ball. As if she were sure of the world and her place in it. As if she were entirely legitimate.

Exactly as Elspeth was not. Just as she had always known.

But there was nothing Elspeth could do about it. The world was the way it was, and sobbing into the underbrush wasn't going to do anything but make her face blotchy. So she stood and smoothed her skirts, and did the only thing she could do—headed home to Dove Cottage.

To the only place here she belonged.

"Is that you, Elspeth?"

At the sound of her aunt's voice, Elspeth was enveloped in all the homey comfort of the familiar, and she wanted nothing more at that moment than to cast herself into their arms. Not that they were great comforters—physical displays of affection being few and far between at Dove Cottage. Still, a kind word could be as comforting as a posset.

Elspeth took a deep breath to try to soften the sharp edges of her feelings of betrayal and hurt. "Yes, Aunt Molly. I'm home."

The Aunts met her at the garden door, standing in front of the portal with their arms linked together for support.

"What is wrong?" Elspeth rushed forward to assist them.

But Aunt Molly drew back, getting to her point with characteristic directness. "We've had the most alarming report, Elspeth, that you were seen consorting with a young man near the orchard this noontide, and then later along the lanes."

"Michty me." Dread tightened in Elspeth's belly like a leather belt drawn too taut. She ought to have known, of course. She ought to have understood that there was no privacy in a village this small—someone was always watching. Someone always reported what they thought they saw.

And things never got better but that they got worse first.

"It was only Mr. Cathcart, Aunt. He and I were talking. And walking. And saying goodbye. He's gone for Edinburgh and his life there."

"You did more than talk if the moss on your collar, and the grass stains on your skirts, and the look of regret in your eye are any indication."

"No, I—" Elspeth half-turned to try and find the moss, and, instead, found a grass stain on her shoulder. Not that she had never innocuously smudged or stained a gown or petticoat working in the garden before, but today, riddy heat seared her cheeks. "I went into the wood by myself, after he left. To…" To have a good cry would be too revealing. "To be alone."

But Aunt Isla wasn't listening—she had been watching Elspeth's hot face. "Well, at least you've the good sense to be mortified by your actions, but I'll tell you this Elspeth Otis, we raised you better than to consort in orchards with the likes of him—a tramp."

"He's not a tramp. I told you, he's Mr. Hamish Cathcart. He's a gentleman."

"Who?" Isla cupped her hand to her ear and then looked to Molly, as if for translation.

"Mr. Cathcart," Elspeth repeated, even as she could feel the telltale heat creep up her neck. "He was only pretending to be a gardener. He's the son of the Earl Cathcart."

"Mr. Cathcart? Son of an earl?" Isla was still confused. "However did you meet him?"

"It makes no nevermind, Elspeth Otis." Aunt Molly held up her hand and closed her eyes, barring any attempt at explanation. "Surely even you are not such a dreamer to imagine that a man of such a fine family would want you for any other reason than to desport himself while ruining you."

"Ruined? I'm not ruined! I'm—" But what was she? Miss Perfect Lorrimer in the lane was his betrothed.

Molly was right—Elspeth was nothing to him. "I'm sorry."

"We're more than sorry, too," Aunt Molly said. "Blood will out, Isla's always said. We tried to raise you right and keep you from iniquity. We did our best—no one can say we didn't—but we won't be made to put up with it, do you hear?" Aunt Molly did not wait for Elspeth's answer, but continued straight on. "We raised you better, Elspeth, and we won't be subject to such…"

"Such licentiousness." Isla supplied the necessary word on a whisper that seemed to take the last of her strength—she swayed and began to crumple toward the floor.

Elspeth was instantly there to catch her, and bear her through the kitchen to the parlor settee.

"No, no," Isla objected. "Don't touch me," she cried. "I want Molly."

"Of course," Elspeth stood back.

"You must go," Molly instructed Elspeth. "Can't you see what you've done?"

Elspeth wouldn't argue that Aunt Isla's palpitations were all her own and not Elspeth's fault, but she knew in her heart she was to blame—Isla was too weak to withstand such a blow to her niece's reputation. "I'll just put the kettle on the hob to make a posset."

"No." Aunt Molly's voice was as emphatic as it was fragile. "You needs must be *gone*."

Her meaning burned Elspeth more deep than any scald from the hob. "Aunts, please." Elspeth tried to speak over her rising panic. "I haven't subjected anyone to any licentious—"

"Don't lie to us, Elspeth. Close up thine mouth before the devil can take any more of your words."

Dread and panic brewed a hissing pot of shame that sealed her mouth. Elspeth recognized the trunk on the other side of the door—its meaning becoming apparent with a sort of searing pain that ripped a hole in her tattered heart.

"As much as it pains us to say"—Molly squared her thin shoulders—"we're done with you, Elspeth. We can't have you here in this house if you're going to behave with such total disregard for the morals and strictures to which you've been raised."

"Can't have me?" Were they casting her out? Now, when they had done all they could, by means fair and foul, to bring her back not a week ago?

The shame and dread were diluted with consternation. And a growing indignation.

"We won't have it, I tell you," Molly was saying. "We won't. We can't have this upset."

The pain leeched out slowly, leaving Elspeth rather numb. "You're putting me out?"

"We are. We must. For your own good." Aunt Molly's wrinkled face was lined with tears. "So you'll realize the value of what you've lost and come to your senses."

"My senses?" Elspeth could hardly believe what she was hearing.

"Aye." Aunt Molly stood quietly firm. "Much as it pains us. You'll have to go."

"Aye then, I will. If you'll be so kind as to let me fetch my cloak and hat." Elspeth didn't wait for their approval, but mounted up the stairs to her room. The sloped ceiling that had only that morning seemed so close and comfortable and warm was now too close and confining. Too small minded.

She snatched up a work bag and threw in only enough to put her on the road to Edinburgh, even if she had to ride in a dray like the castoff she was meant to be.

She could only pray that Aunt Augusta would still take her in.

Chapter 25

HAMISH EXTRICATED HIMSELF as politely, but forthrightly as possible from the Lorrimers' claims. "You were right to come here, Mr. Lorrimer, for things are most definitely not right and tight. In fact, they are entirely havey-cavey, if my family has entered into any agreements or marriage contract with you."

"They have done so!" the bullish brewer confirmed.

"They have not the right, for I am of age, and I am not free to become engaged." Hamish straightened his coat, and stood himself up tall. "For you see, I am already married."

This proclamation was met, for the moment, with stunned silence.

The brewer and his heiress looked at each other with something more powerful and more personal than either anger or regret. "To the dairy maid?" Miss Lorrimer, who was clearly not stupid, asked.

"To my wife." Hamish let some heat raise his voice. "Whom I will not allow you to disparage."

"No, forgive me." Miss Lorrimer amended to cover her incredulity. "I saw nothing in the newspapers, or we should never have come. Never contemplated—"

"Of course." Hamish eased his own tone. "It has not yet been put in." Mostly because it had not yet happened, but that was a minor detail he would arrange forthwith. "Nevertheless, I want to make it clear that we"—he indicated Miss Lorrimer and himself—"are not engaged, nor will we ever be married. And I would appreciate it greatly if my name and that of my wife were not put about."

"Of course not." She pursed her lips and looked away to conceal her embarrassment or her hurt—he could not tell which. "Though I hope I have given you no reason to think I would do such a thing."

It was Hamish's turn to be chagrinned, and he realized that Miss Lorrimer had her own, different disappointments than either Elspeth or himself—he could, and would at his first opportunity, find Elspeth and make all right between them. Miss Lorrimer, with her trade-earned fortune and her brewer of a father, would have a harder time finding herself a new prospect for a husband.

"I hope you take no offense to yourself, Miss Lorrimer. I regret deeply that this misunderstanding has happened, and would have been honored to act upon my family's wishes were I not already quite taken—contracted, married and very much in love with another."

Hamish had meant the admission to be for Miss Lorrimer, to salve her pride and wounded feelings, but the moment he said it, Hamish knew truer words he had never spoken— Elsepth was his only love. His light and his one true match in the world.

And speak those words again he needed to—posthaste. "If you'll excuse me, Miss Lorrimer, Mr. Lorrimer." He bowed and turned on his heels. "I have most urgent business I must attend to."

With Fergus's adroit assistance Hamish was dressed in a suitably gentlemanly suit of clothes, seated upon a hunter of more aristocratic bloodlines than his own, and ready to present himself to the ladies of Dove Cottage whereupon he would soothe the upset of the morning, and plight his troth.

But the ladies of Dove Cottage were more militant than he expected—they would not answer the bell at their door, even though he could hear them, talking between themselves inside.

So Hamish took himself to the window. "Dear ladies, I have come to make my peace and make my honorable intentions known to you. But I cannot do so through a closed door."

"Begone," the cried from within, "or we'll set the dog on you."

"Dear ladies, you haven't got a dog." Hamish was sure he would have noticed such a beast in the days prior. This was just a vain attempt to test him, and he wasn't about to be put off. Not now, when his happiness was so close. "Will you not hear me out? I don't particularly want to propose through a window, but I will. I love Elspeth enough that I don't mind *how* I ask for the honor of her hand."

The silence that met this proposal would have been deafening but for the fact that he was in a country lane, where it was never really quiet—the hedgerows fairly rattled with all manner of answers.

"But we don't *know* you," was finally the plaintive response.

"Then let me introduce myself properly, ladies. I am Mr. Hamish Cathcart of Edinburgh, son of the Earl Cathcart of Renfrewshire, and other various and assorted places that I am sure he would be glad and proud to tell you about, but which bore me to tears. Because the point of this visit is to assure you that though my fortune is currently small, it is independent, and I have every confidence that I will increase it if you will do me the honor of letting Miss Elspeth Otis become by helpmeet and wife, and be by my side."

It was a rather long, rambling sort of proposal, but Hamish was pleased and proud of it, for he meant never to make another. Though he did not yet appear to be finished with this one.

One of the sisters Murray made a rattle of unlatching the door, peering around the portal to consider him. "I don't care if you're the Earl Cathcart or the King of England, himself. But I suppose you look well enough like a gentleman."

"I hope I am that, ma'am, in deed as well as appearance."

She opened the door and stood aside. "I suppose you had better come in."

Hamish was careful to wipe his boots, and take off his hat so as not to dirty the floor, nor crowd the ceiling of the snug little cottage. He bowed to the two tiny sisters. "Thank you for seeing me. I am honored."

The smaller of the two ladies pursed her lips in disagreement. "We didn't want the neighbors to see you standing in the garden like a scarecrow."

A well-dressed, aristocratic scarecrow. "Nay, mistress. That would never do."

"It won't. And I'll tell you another thing that won't do," the door minder averred. "You had no business turning our poor Elspeth's head and filling it with empty promises."

"My promise is not empty," he tried to assure her. "I would deem it an honor and a privilege if she would consent to be my wife."

"You can't mean that. This is some ruse to—"

"No ruse. Let me do all I can to convince you of my sincerity, ma'am. I love and admire and esteem your niece, and I should be the happiest of men were you to honor us with your blessing, for it would mean so much to her. But I will tell you, that I mean to have her to wife, whether you give your blessing or not. We are both of age. And this is Scotland. And"—he threw one last piece of fuel on the fire—"we are handfasted, and so engaged."

The two old women shared a glance that seemed relieved, if not impressed. "Have you the backing of your family?" the older and taller one asked.

Hamish would not dishonor Elspeth's family by lying. "I belong to an ancient and honorable family, Miss Murray, but my own name and my own character are all I can offer your niece. I hope that they are enough to secure your approval."

"She's a bastard." The smaller of the two ladies thrust the accusation at him like a sword.

But he had weapons of his own—a shield of righteous anger and steadfast love. "Elspeth may be illegitimate, but bastardy is not a part of her character." He worked to keep the steel from his voice. "And I will not have that word spoken in reference to her again. Do I make myself clear?"

In silence the sisters Murray looked at each other in silent communication before they turned to him. "At last. My dear Mr. Cathcart, we could not give her to you if you felt otherwise."

Relief slid slowly into his veins like a cool bath, calming him, and firming his resolve. "Then all that remains is for me to plight my troth to Elspeth. Where is she?"

Another long speaking look passed between the women before the older of the two spoke. "We're afraid she's gone, Mr. Cathcart. We are ashamed to say we drove her out, and can only hope that she is gone to her Aunt Ivers in Edinburgh."

Hamish withstood the disappointment of delayed gratification with all the sanguinity he could muster. Which was considerable—he was a man who knew how to make new plans. "Then I think, my dear aunts, that we had best get you two packed for Edinburgh."

Chapter 26

ELSPETH WAS TIRED and footsore by the time she made St. Andrew Square, for she had walked a long way past the next village before she had found a farmer's dray heading for Edinburgh's Grass Market. But her spirits were revived when Aunt Augusta opened the door herself.

"My darling girl!" Augusta enveloped her in a tight, heartfelt embrace. "Oh, it is so lovely to have you back. We have so much to do. I am so very, very excited and pleased—" She took another look at Elspeth's face. "But what is wrong? Where is Hamish?" She peered over Elspeth's shoulder. "I thought he was gone to find you. Where is he?"

Instead of breaking into tears—as she had already done at more than one point upon her journey, Elspeth chose to be angry. "Gone to the devil for all I know—he did not deign to come. I left him with his betrothed." Elspeth curbed her bitterness and firmed her resolve. "As for me, I've come to Edinburgh to be a wastrel, just like my father. Blood will out, the Aunts said, so here I am."

Instead of gasping in shock as she might have expected, Lady Augusta took only a moment before she broke into a smile so wide and bright, Elspeth might have put out her chilled hands to the warmth.

"You must tell me what happened, but bless them for

being so stupidly missish." Aunt Augusta clasped her hand to lead her upward to the drawing room. "Their loss is my gain. And your father was a wastrel only because he wasted his gifts—squandered on women of no character and wine of little distinction in the terrible grief of the loss of your mother. And you, my darling brave girl, will never do that."

"I thank you for your enthusiastic and unwavering confidence, Aunt Augusta, but the unhappy truth of the matter is that I find myself in an awful pickle."

"And by awful pickle," that kind lady asked gently, "do you mean you've fallen quite in love with Hamish?"

It was a long moment before Elspeth trusted herself to speak clearly. "I suppose I do. More or less." It was all so complicated and sad. She had thought she loved him, most fervently. But now she was angry as well as sad. "But before I can allow myself to throw over Hamish Cathcart, that man needs to be taught a lesson."

"Oh, yes." Lady Augusta clasped her hands together in fervent agreement. "How entirely delightful. I don't know how a man as besotted as Hamish Cathcart came to make such a hash of things, but I offer you my full and wickedly experienced assistance on the instant."

The time, Elspeth could not stop the tears that pooled in her eyes. "Thank you, dear Aunt."

"Yes, yes. But we must act quickly, at once!" She drew Elspeth to her in a fierce embrace. "Oh, I knew I should grow to love you, now more than ever before." She clapped her hands together, immediately calling for the butler. "Reeves, call all the staff immediately. As my dearest Admiral Ivers would have said, pipe all hands to battle stations!"

Battle stations turned out to be a great deal more comfortable that Elspeth might have thought. "My niece needs must be cosseted," her Aunt Augusta declared.

And cosseted, Elspeth was—she was soaked in a bath hot enough to soothe her aches, and fed until she was well past sated, and put to bed so tired that she fell directly into a dreamless sleep.

And in the morning, the battle order was redrawn—

Elspeth was bathed and coiffed and fed and dressed in a gown of cerulean blue silk that shimmered and whispered encouragement when she walked.

It was almost enough to give her confidence that life would go on much less disastrously than she might have thought, or had any right to expect.

"Perfection," Aunt Augusta decreed as her dresser put the finishing touches on Elspeth's ensemble. "Pure, absolute perfection. Nothing more—her head bare and honest. Yes,"—she stood back to peruse Elspeth once more—"you'll do perfectly."

"Do for what, Aunt Augusta?"

"The occasion," the lady answered, as if that explained anything. "Battle armor, as it were, though I should think it safe to say you have already won the war."

"What war?"

Aunt Augusta favored her with that mischievous smile that carved dimples deep into her cheeks. "All in good time, my darling. And it is time"—she picked up her own silk skirts and proceeded to the door—"for us to go."

"To where, pray?"

"To church." She swept down the steps and into the waiting carriage.

Elspeth felt heat sweep her cheeks. But after missing kirk yesterday, perhaps it was right that she attend divine services, and take a quiet hour to reflect and forgive herself the passions and mistakes of the past, as well as seek some divine guidance on what she ought to do next.

Working with Mr. Hamish Cathcart was out of the question, of course. Aunt Augusta was going to be so disappointed.

But Aunt Augusta was fussing with the fall of her niece's lace. "It must look just so."

"But it is a Monday morning," Elspeth objected. "Is there some holy day that I did not know existed?"

"There is indeed," Aunt Augusta said tartly. "Now get yourself into the carriage, and say not another word."

They had not far to go, only around the corner onto

George Street, whereupon the carriage pulled up in front of the high-clocked steeple of St. Andrew's kirk.

Where *he* was waiting beneath the tall columned portico— her Mr. Hamish Cathcart, looking as tall and mischievous and Scots as ever she might have imagined.

Aunt Augusta took her elbow to urge her down to the pavement, but Elspeth did not know whether to gape or cry—she had just been thinking ill of him, but here he was, smiling at her as if she were the fairest and finest thing in the world.

He was dressed in the old style, in the distinct blue, red and green plaid of the Clan Cathcart tartan, with a sword hung at his side. He was breathtaking and impressive. And confusing.

And what was more confusing was the way Hamish offered her his hand, and wordlessly led her into the kirk, past the astonishing sight of the Aunts Murray, smiling wistfully and dabbing at their damp eyes with familiar worn lace-edged handkerchiefs.

Past the Countess of Inverness smiling contentedly. Past Aunt Augusta, who slipped into the pew with the countess, looking entirely too pleased with herself.

"Just as you are," Aunt Augusta whispered, as Hamish swept Elspeth past on the way to the altar, where a rosy-cheeked rector peered down his glasses at her.

"We're all assembled then?" the white-robed cleric asked. "Are we ready to begin?"

"Elspeth?" Hamish finally spoke. "Are we ready?"

"Nay."

"Elspeth—"

"What of your Miss Lorrimer and her brewery?" she asked as quietly as she could in a place that echoed so monstrously.

"A misunderstanding. A great, unnecessary misunderstanding that has delayed my making you my wife."

It hadn't felt like a misunderstanding—it had felt like her heart had been rent in two. And hearts could not so easily be put back together.

She wanted assurances. "I really wish you had proposed

to me properly before such a misapprehension took place, Hamish."

"Then let me propose to you again, now, my love."

"Properly, Hamish," she insisted. "Down on one knee before everyone and God, the way you ought to have done at the start."

"I couldn't have done so at the start," he reasoned teasingly, "as I hardly knew you."

"You know what I mean." Elspeth held her ground—she would start as she meant to go on. "I want a proper declaration of love from you, Hamish Cathcart. And I want it now, or we go no further."

If anything, Hamish's smile grew wider, spilling across his face like mischief. "Then you shall have it. My darling Miss Otis," he began, going down on the cold, slate floor on one bare knee. "I beg you to make me the happiest of men, by doing me the honor of accepting my unworthy proposal for your hand."

It was a pretty enough start. But not enough. "Why?"

"Because without you, my life and my world would be a poorer place. Because I love you with all my heart and all my mind and all my soul, and I do not want to face another dawn of waking up without you."

Elspeth felt a rightness, a warmth settle upon her like a ray of sunshine beaming down through the windows. A benediction, as it were—a feeling that finally, at last, all was right with her world.

A feeling that she was home at last.

"That's better." She gave him her hand.

He raised her palm to his lips. "Is that a yes?"

"Nay, it's an aye."

The rector cleared his throat and began, "Dearly beloved brethren, we are here gathered together in the sight of God, and in the face of His congregation to knit and join these parties together in the honorable estate of matrimony—"

Epilogue

HAMISH TOOK HER home to Cathcart Lodge, of course, tucked away in the quiet hills. There was nowhere else where she would feel so at home but in her native country. And yet the quiet lodge was still private enough that they would not have to see anyone from her village for a week if they so chose. And they did not so choose.

They chose to lie naked hour after hour in a soft, comfortable bed, with the windows wide open to the fragrant summer air. They made love through rainstorms and sun squalls, through chilly mornings and warm afternoons. They talked and ate and loved and rewrote her father's book without ever leaving the bed.

And Elspeth had never, ever been happier. "Have I thanked you properly?"

"For what," he asked, pulling her closer to lie atop his lovely naked chest.

"For making me write books, and marrying me, and making me so happy."

"We make ourselves happy, my darling heart, when we are true to ourselves." He kissed her forehead. "And it was really your Aunt Augusta who made you write books."

"Aunt Augusta and, perhaps, the ghost of my father."

"Pray don't talk of fathers, my sweet, when I am intent

upon ravishing his daughter."

Elspeth felt her smile spread across her face until it became a laugh. "I think my father, of all men, would approve."

"And I approve of his daughter, most heartily."

"Love me, Hamish Cathcart. Give me another one of your lessons in kissing."

He rolled her onto her back, and gave her that smile that said he would lead her into mischief. "My darling Elspeth. Wouldn't you prefer a lesson in a great deal more?"

She did. And she always would. It was in her blissfully tainted blood.

Thank You for Reading

Thank you for reading *A Fine Madness*. I hope you'll take a few minutes out of your day to review this book – your honest opinion is much appreciated. Reviews help introduce readers to new authors they wouldn't otherwise meet.
Review here

The Highland Brides

A Fine Madness is the third book in the Highland Brides series. While each romance reads as a stand-alone, the series is best enjoyed in chronological order.

Mad for Love
Mad About the Marquess
A Fine Madness
Mad, Bad, and Dangerous to Marry – coming soon
Mad Dogs and Englishmen – coming soon

To keep up to date on The Highland Brides, sign up for Elizabeth's newsletter and get exclusive excerpts, contests, and more
http://eepurl.com/bQgwk9

**Read on for an excerpt from
Mad About the Marquess*!***

LADY QUINCE WINTHROP had always known she was the unfortunate sort of lass who could resist everything but temptation. And the man across the ballroom was temptation in a red velvet coat. There was something about him—some aura of English arrogance, some presumption of privilege—that tempted her beyond reason, beyond caution, and beyond sense. Something that tempted her to steal from him. Right there in the Countess of Inverness's ballroom. In the middle of the ball.

Which was entirely out of character. Not the stealing—she stole as naturally as she breathed. But because the other thing that Lady Quince Winthrop had always known, was that the most important thing about stealing was not *where* one relieved a person of his valuable chattels. Nor *when*. Nor *how*. Nor even *what* particular wee trinket one slipped into one's hidden pockets. Nay.

The tricky bit was always *from whom* one stole.

When one robbed from the rich, one had to be careful. Pick the wrong man, or woman for that matter—too canny, too important, too powerful—and even the perfect plan could collapse as completely as a plum custard in a cupboard. Which made it all the more curious when she ignored her own advice, and picked the wrong man anyway.

Whoever he was, he stood with his back to her, his white-powdered hair in perfect contrast to that red velvet coat so vivid and plush and enticing that Quince was drawn to it like a Spanish bull to a bright swirling cape. Unlike the gaudily embroidered suits worn by the other men, the crimson coat was entirely unadorned but for two gleaming silver buttons that winked at her in the candlelight, practically begging her to nip one of the expensive little embellishments right off his back.

A button like that could feed a family of six for a fortnight.

And while her itchy-fingered tendency toward theft was

perhaps not the most sterling of characteristics in an otherwise well brought up young Scotswoman, no one was perfect. And it was so very hard to be *good* all the time.

She had much rather be bad, and be *right*.

So Quince took advantage of the terrific crush in Lady Inverness's ballroom, slipped her finger into the tiny ring knife she kept secreted in the muslin folds of her bodice for just such an occasion, and sidled up behind Crimson Velvet.

She did not pause, nor give herself a moment to think on what she was about to do. She ignored the chitter of warning racing across her skin, and set straight to it, diverting his attention by brushing her bodice quite purposefully against his back, while she nipped the button off as easily as if it were a snap pea in a garden.

The elation was like a rush of blood to the head—intoxicating and addictive.

And because that was what she did—regularly stole fine things from finer people in the finest of ballrooms—she wasn't satisfied with only the one button. Nay. Another six mouths could be fed, and Quince could live all week on the illicit thrill of having taken the second button as well, and gotten away clean.

Except that she didn't get away clean.

She didn't get away at all.

A very large hand clamped onto Quince's wrist like a shackle. A red velvet-clad hand.

Alarm jumped onto her chest like a sharp-clawed cat, but Quince kept her head, automatically tucking the buttons and knife down the front of her bodice, and winding her now-empty free hand around that crimson velvet waist. She pressed herself to his backside more firmly, and familiarly, and said the first unexpected thing that came to her mind. "Darling!"

Crimson Velvet went as stiff as a bottle of Scotch whisky. "Good Lord. What's this?"

Alarm faded as recognition, and something that really oughtn't be delight curled into her veins. She knew that deceptively easy tone. Strathcairn. Earl thereof.

Oh, holy clotted cream.

The Laughing Highlander, she had once called him. But the Highlander was not laughing now. He was looking down at her with a sort of astonished wonder. "Wee Quince Winthrop, is that you? Good Lord." He stepped away— though he did not let go of her wrist—to case her as thoroughly as she ought to have done him. "I would not have recognized you."

She had clearly not recognized him. But the man gripping her wrist was neither the powdered dandy she had imagined from across the ballroom, nor the amusing, carefree Earl of Strathcairn she remembered. This man was different, and as dazzling in his own way as the shining silver buttons she had secreted down her soft-pleated bodice.

Firstly, he was as irresistibly attractive as that red velvet suit—all precise, well-cut shoulders, and long lean torso that seemed a far cry from the rangy, not-yet-fully-formed man in his youth. But secondly—and more importantly—he was much more controlled, more…curated, as if he had carefully chosen this particularly splendid view of himself to show the world. As if he not only wanted, but demanded to be *seen*.

Quite the opposite of Quince, who minded her appearance only to make sure she blended into the crowd— if her sister told her this season everyone was wearing white chemise dresses, then a white chemise dress she wore, disappearing into a sea of similarly dressed swans.

By contrast, Strathcairn looked every bit an individual, and quite, quite splendid. His waistcoat was of the same saturated color as his coat, and his snow-bright linen with only the barest hint of lace was the perfect foil for his immaculately powdered hair.

On any other man such a look might have appeared plain and underdone, but on Strathcairn the blaze of unadorned velvet served to highlight the force of his personality.

And there was nothing she liked as much as personality, unless it was a challenge.

The earl appeared to be both.

"Why, Strathcairn." She made her voice everything breezy

and cordial. As if her heart were not beating in her ears, and dangerous delight were not dancing down her veins. "It's been an age."

"Too long, from the looks of it." He stepped close—too close, not that she particularly minded—and looked down at her in a perilously attentive way, like a great, green-eyed tomcat eyeing up a wee mouse. The effect was most unsettling. It put her right off her stride. "Do you often embrace men you haven't seen in years?"

It had been exactly five years. He had briefly been one of her eldest sister Linnea's suitors then—newly elected a Member of Parliament, and headed to London, brilliant and ambitious. Quince remembered thinking the lanky Highlander was too tall, too clever, too canny, and far too insightful for tiny, fluttery Linnea, who adored nothing more than to be made a pet of.

Strathcairn hadn't seemed the type to keep pets.

Quince had been little more than a fourteen-year-old lass, but she had quite liked the young man's intelligence, nearly as much as his vibrant charm. Though what she liked best of all was his lovely, buttery smile that had made her feel like she was melting in the sun.

Strathcairn was certainly not pouring the butter boat over her now—his eyes might have been smiling, but from this angle, his chiseled jaw seemed to have been carved out of Grampian granite.

No matter. Quince was not Linnea—she was no one's pet. "I thought you were someone else," she lied without effort or qualm. "You've changed."

"So, my indiscreet young friend, have you." The barest hint of amusement in his glorious baritone was all that was necessary to bring back all the delicious torment of her youthful infatuation. "What in heaven's name did you think you were doing, calling me 'darling'?"

"Thought you were my Davie." Quince made up a convenient beau on the spot. "I must find where the darling lad's got to."

Strathcairn let out a low, disbelieving bark of laughter, but didn't let go of her wrist. "You can't be old enough to be making assignations with men, wee Quince."

He trespassed easily on the old acquaintance by calling her by her Christian name—if Papa's botanically inspired names for his daughters could even be called Christian. Strathcairn also crossed the lines of familiar behavior by turning her toward the door, and somehow settling her against his side in such a subtle, but insistent, way, that not a person in the place would have suspected she was being all but frog-marched from the ballroom.

Even though she was grown up now, and towered over tiny Linnea, Quince still had to leg it to keep up with Strathcairn's long strides, all the while craning her neck to get a proper close look at him.

He looked so different, with his hair powdered white, and this controlled look upon his face, as if his smile had been put away in a cupboard, like a cravat that no longer fit. This new Strathcairn was far more imposing, and much, much more intimidating looming beside her like one of the great statues at Holyrood Palace than he had ever seemed all those years ago when she had keeked out at him from behind the drawing room curtains.

But she was not four and ten now. Quince let him tow her only as far as a conveniently empty alcove at the end of the entrance hall, before she rounded her elbow out of his grip, and served him a sharp, instructive jab in the ribs—anger brought out the Scots in her. "I'd be much obliged if you'd take your great paws off of me, Strathcairn. You're creasing my gown."

He subdued his grunt of discomfort, but put a hand absently to his side. "My *paws*"—he gave the word a wry intonation—"are not great in the least. They're rather average. For a Scot." At last he let the gorgeously rough Scots burr rumble beneath the town polish of his Member-of-Parliament accent. "Your gown is barely creased, and not by me, but by that interminable crush. Or more likely by this Davie fellow. And who the devil is he?" Strathcairn's green gaze poured over her like chilly water. "He can't possibly be a worthy mon if he lets a lass like you caress him in public. You're too young for suitors."

By jimble, but he had grown into an even more attractive man himself over the years, despite this polished, urbane facade. Or perhaps because of it—his worldliness gave him an attractive look of experienced wisdom. Quite irresistible.

"I'm not young anymore, either. I'm nineteen."

This he acknowledged with a wry sideways slant of his head, as if she were so out of kilter that the acute angle somehow made it easier to see her. "A very bad age to be an accomplished liar. And flirt." Strathcairn finally released her arm.

Much to her chagrin—which was all the emotion she would allow to account for the strange warmth suffusing her face—she found she missed the contact. How disconcerting.

So she changed the subject. Without flirting. "What are you doing in Edinburgh?"

"I've come north to see to Castle Cairn now that my grandfather's passed on."

Something that must have been sincerity stabbed her hard in the chest. "I am sorry, Strathcairn. He was a grand auld gent."

It was the right thing to say—Strathcairn's whole demeanor softened enough to show her more of the young man she had admired beneath his curated veneer. Even those glittering eyes went soft at the edges. "Thank you. He was, wasn't he?"

"Aye." The Marquess of Cairn had been a cavalier of the old school, gentlemanly, generous and bold. He had raised Strathcairn when his son, Strathcairn's father and the prior earl, had passed away suddenly during Straithcairn's youth. "He'll be missed. Oh—that means you're Cairn now."

Strathcairn—for she could think of him no other way even if he were now Marquess of Cairn—lowered that chiseled chin, and nodded in rueful agreement. "Aye. And he's left large boots to fill. So I'm seeing to Cairn." He took a deep breath as if he were collecting himself before he raised his head, and added, "But before I head north to home, I've also been asked to see to a rather persistent problem plaguing Edinburgh."

A softer sense of alarm—or perhaps it was guilt—padded across her shoulders like a stealthy barn cat. She made light of it, as she always did. "The persistent plague of too many ladies and not enough gentlemen? I do hope you've come prepared to dance."

The first hint of a smile began at the far corner of his lips, as if he were not yet ready to commit to the strenuous exercise of a full-out grin. "No. I rarely dance." He shook his head in rueful apology. "No, the problem I speak of is a rash of thefts from some of the better households in the district. I've been asked to restore some sense of law and order within Edinburgh's society."

"On guard" was too simple and sensible a phrase to describe her reaction—Quince's skin went a little cold, and that sharp-clawed sense of alarm scratched its way down her spine. But she rose to the occasion—she knew better than most how to put up her weapons. To win any sort of fight, one had to attack, not just defend. And satire was the sharpest sword of them all.

"*Restore* law and order?" She made herself suitably wide-eyed and breathless. "I hadn't realized we were lacking it. Ought we to be on watch for gangs of housebreakers?"

"No, no. Nothing like that." He looked sage and worldly with all his unruffled calm, but she could see a tinge of riddy heat creeping over his collar. "Though it's too early to tell. But certainly too early for worry. Pray don't be alarmed, lass."

Quince's skin went all over prickly—nothing put her back up like being condescended to.

She sharpened up her sarcasm so he would not be able to so easily evade her point. "Holy sticky toffee pudding, Strathcairn"—she decided if he could trespass upon her Christian name, then she would trespass upon his old title—"imagine that. A gang of cutthroat housebreakers carting off priceless *Louis Quatorze* commodes to furnish their tatty tenement houses. How have the newspapers and broadsheets not been full of that?"

His smile confined itself to the outer corners of those intelligent green eyes. "No priceless commodes have been carted off."

"Auld occasional tables, then? Scaffy, mismatched chairs?"

"You needn't mock, lass. It's not ladylike." He put a hand up to rub the back of his neck, as if she really were succeeding in making him uncomfortable. Marvelous. And he had to subdue his growing smile—it started to hitch up one side of his mouth, as if he wanted to be amused, but was sure he oughtn't be. "If you must know, it's been very small items—smelling salt bottles, buttons, and the like."

And her with his two buttons down her bodice. She could feel them press into her skin as if they were biting her. Unsurprising since they were *his*.

Quince was too larky a lass to let a bit of her discomfort show. "Really? You've never abandoned Westminster, and come all the way north from London for some missing smelling salts?"

He had the good nature to look chagrined—that wary smile turned down sheepishly at the corners. "Not exactly. It's more complicated than that."

In fact, it was a great deal simpler than that. And she could not resist telling him so. "Well, it's a very good thing you told *me*." She lowered her voice in mock confidence. "Because I'm sure I know exactly what's happened to them."

He did not lean down to share her confidences. If anything, he became more upright, and even tilted away from her, as if he thought he could see her better from a distance. "You, lass?"

"Aye." She seized him by the upper arms, and manhandled him around—and by jimble if he hadn't the brawest, most firmly shaped musculature hidden under that soft, plush velvet—so he could follow the direction of her gaze. "There. Mr. Fergus McElmore has misplaced his snuffbox there, right under that vase of heather and broom. See? And there"—she pushed him in the other direction—"the Dowager Countess of Chester has abandoned her silver vinaigrette bottle in the cushion of her seat. Q.E.D. as you parliamentary types say." She made a dramatic flourish as if she were a theatrical barrister in court. "There is the *modus operandi* of your thefts, Strathcairn—silly stupidity at worst, simple thoughtlessness at best. Though in Fergus' case particularly, I think the thoughtlessness has come from an excess of Lady Inverness's fine Scotch whisky befuddling his poor wee numptie brain."

A fine coloring heat crept up Strathcairn's neck to his jawline. It lessened that impression of Grampian granite nicely.

He shook his head, but smiled nonetheless. "You think me foolish."

"I think whoever complained of their missing baubles is foolish, when they are likely only victims of their own excess—how *can* they be expected to keep track of so many possessions?"

He looked at her then—really looked, as if he finally saw more of her than the ghost of her pigtailed past. "You've a remarkably jaundiced view of society for a lass your age."

She was more than jaundiced. She was nearly lock-jawed with disdain. "I have a realistic understanding of human nature, Strathcairn. I think people are forgetful, and don't want to appear foolish, so they bluster and blame others for their own mistakes. And it is easy enough to blame the powerless"—she nodded toward the servants, who were most often the first to be accused when anything went amiss—"from the safe position of privilege."

"I take your meaning, lass." He acknowledged the right of her argument with a nod. "Nevertheless, it is my duty to look into the matter, to determine if it is indeed only a case—or cases—of forgetfulness."

"Then I should advise you to start with our hostess, and ask her what she does with all the flotsam and jetsam her guests leave behind after her balls." Because not even Quince, terrible magpie that she was, could take everything that was available—her bodice could only hold so much. "Perhaps she has the footmen cart it all up, and take it to the poor box at Canongate Kirk where they'll get better use of it."

The moment the words were out of her mouth she wished them back. She'd let her tongue run away from her mind, and run far too close to the truth for comfort.

And her suggestion brought Strathcairn's perilously attentive green gaze back to her. "What an agile mind you have, Lady Quince." And then for no reason she could fathom, he smiled at her—that gorgeous, gleaming grin she remembered of old. That mischievous, sideways curve of lip that made her feel as if she were being blessedly bludgeoned over the head with a five-penny slab of butter.

Quince nearly had to pinch herself to call her wits back under starter's orders. "Oh, pish tosh. Practical is what my mind is."

His smile settled back down to the corner of those sharp eyes. "Perhaps, but you've given me an idea—perhaps what I'm looking for is not a hardened criminal, but someone with the dowagers's vice."

Nay, nay, nay.

Clever, too clear-eyed man.

She had to divert him with something equally clever. "Carrying a vinaigrette is a vice? What do you imagine the ladies keep in there? Undiluted opium?"

Strathcairn shook his head, but he was amused enough to still smile. "The dowager's vice is the irresistible tendency toward theft. That is, the compulsive stealing of objects which are not rightfully theirs. It is commonly practiced by maiden aunties and elderly companions. And dowagers, of course. Hence the name."

Oh, by jimble. That sounded far too apt.

And the skeptical Scot in him had taken over—he was frowning at the row of seats at the far side of the ballroom where the older ladies, including some rather impecunious relations and companions, sat with their heads together in a comfortable coze. "They look perfectly harmless, but one never knows what might be hidden in their reticules, or tucked into their bodices."

Heat blossomed in that very place where Strathcairn's purloined buttons dug into her skin. Oh, he was clever.

But so was she. "Down their bodices?" She quite purposefully, and quite inexpertly, straightened her trim bodice, drawing his attention out the side of his eye to her small, but nevertheless eminently serviceable breasts. Mama always said a man couldn't think and look at breasts, no matter their size. No fool, Mama. And the clever padding Mama had insisted her maid sew into her stays made up for any natural deficit. "How do they find any room? Must be dreadful uncomfortable."

His brow rose as slowly as a guillotine over that acute eye. But his self-control was not equal to the task at hand, and his gaze strayed exactly where she had meant it to.

"Lady Quince." Strathcairn's lowered voice was absolutely irresistible when he forgot himself enough to let the Scots burr rumble. "Let me make right sure I understand you—are you *flirting* with me?"

"Am I?" Quince ignored the blaze of heat his voice and gaze kindled under her skin, and gave him her bright, knowing smile—all pleased lips and mischievous eyes. "What I am doing is trying to make you remember your duty, and accede to my wish to dance with me."

He regarded her with those too canny, too bright green eyes for another long moment before he answered. "Perhaps I will." He reached for her hand, and held her at arm's length for a lengthy perusal, as if he had not yet decided to grant her wish. "Yes, I definitely will. But before I do so, perhaps I ought to warn you, wee Quince, to be good. And be very, very careful what you wish for."

The heat that had blossomed under her bodice spread like wildflowers across her skin along the whole length of his gaze. And she liked it.

She raised her chin and gave him her slyest smile yet. "Oh, I am always careful, Strathcairn. But I had much rather be bad, and be *right*."

ABOUT THE AUTHOR

Elizabeth Essex is the award-winning author of the critically acclaimed Reckless Brides historical romance series. When not rereading Jane Austen, mucking about in her garden or simply messing about with boats, Elizabeth can be always be found with her laptop, making up stories about heroes and heroines who live far more exciting lives than she. It wasn't always so. Long before she ever set pen to paper, Elizabeth graduated from Hollins College with a BA in Classics and Art History, and then earned her MA in Nautical Archaeology from Texas A&M University. While she loved the life of an underwater archaeologist, she has found her true calling writing lush, lyrical historical romance full of passion, daring and adventure.

Elizabeth lives in Texas with her husband, the indispensable Mr. Essex, and her active and exuberant family in an old house filled to the brim with books.

Elizabeth loves to hear from readers, so please feel free to contact her at the following places:
E-mail: elizabeth@elizabethessex.com
Web: http://elizabethessex.com
Twitter: https://twitter.com/EssexRomance
Facebook Page:
https://www.facebook.com/elizabeth.essex.37
Pinterest: https://www.pinterest.com/elizabethessex/
Goodreads:
http://www.goodreads.com/author/show/4070364.Elizabeth_Essex